This book is for my mother,
in praise of her spirit,
her generosity.

CONTENTS

FAT MONROE   1

THE FAVOR   11

NIGHT RIDE   23

THE FIGHT   41

THE TAIL-END OF
YESTERDAY   57

HOME FOR THE
WEEKEND   67

THE REVIVAL   77

THE WOUNDED MAN   87

MAXINE   99

A CORRESPONDENCE   109

FAT MONROE

The boy walked on the right side of the road the first mile or two, trying to hitch a ride home after seeing the show in town.

But it was late Saturday afternoon and most of the folks from his end of the county who'd been to town that day had already gone on home.

Only two cars passed him in two miles and they didn't even slow down.

So finally he gave up trying to thumb, crossed the narrow pike to the higher shoulder where the walking was better and stepped out at his best pace toward home.

But then he didn't get a hundred yards before a dusty pickup rattled past him, slowed, stopped, then came flying down the highway backwards, straddling the white dividing line.

"Well hurry up there boy!" shouted a big fat man with a cigar between his teeth. "I'm losing air in both front tires, running out of gas plus an airplane's going to land here any minute now. Come on!"

The boy was already running but at the sound of the man's hoarse voice he ran faster. He knew better than to believe that about the airplane but he glanced into the sky anyway as he climbed on the running board. And for something to do in the awkward first moment in the cab, he craned his neck and through the windshield looked at the sky again.

"Take either one of those seats there you want, old timer," the fat man said, shifting gears as the old truck started rolling. "I wouldn't want you to be uncomfortable."

There was so much junk on the seat and the floor the boy barely found room for himself, and that was on the point of a spring sticking through the cotton wadding and imitation leather of the seat. Around him were tools and parts of two or three old motors, a chainsaw and a can of gasoline, some steel cable and a great coil of thick rope on the floor. The boy glanced at the man curiously, then out at the sky again. Finally he settled back with his feet propped on a tool box.

"Well, what is it?" the fat man asked.

"What's what?" asked Wilgus.

"Your name. What is it? Puddintane?"

"Wilgus Collier," said the boy.

"How was that again?" said the man. He cupped his hand to his ear and leaned in Wilgus' direction. "This old truck makes so much noise I don't hear good."

"Wilgus Collier."

The fat man nodded. "Monroe Short. That's what I thought you said. But I wonder if that's actually right. I mean, could your name be Short Monroe and you just got confused?"

Wilgus grinned. "My name's Wilgus Collier," he said.

"Just like that, eh? Monroe Short and that's all?"

"Wilgus Collier's my name. I don't have a middle name."

The fat man shook his head and sucked his teeth. "Well," he said. "Either way, it's a poor out for a name. What I mean, it's not any name you'd go around bragging about. Why don't you change it, call yourself Monroe, or Stepinfetchit or something?"

Wilgus laughed out loud this time. "Oh, I'll just keep it like it is."

The fat man shrugged. "Well," he said. "It's a free country. How about a cigar?"

He reached into a box of cigars next to his leg and took out three or four. He put all but one into his shirt pocket, then held the one out for Wilgus.

3

Wilgus said he didn't smoke.

"That's all right," said the fat man. "Take it home and give it to your mommy. Or sell it to somebody if nothing else. That's something you ought to learn, Short Collier, don't never turn down a free cigar. Besides, it would be a kindness to me if you took it."

"Well, okay," said Wilgus, and he held out his hand. "Give me one then."

Looking very solemn and earnest, the man put the good cigar in his shirt pocket with the others, then took the frayed, soggy one out of his mouth and ceremoniously stuck it in Wilgus' hand.

"Yes sir," he said. " I learned a long time ago about not taking stuff that's free. It's like I said to my wives, I got 'em all together one day . . . but you probably don't want to hear that story. Tell me, Monroe, how many wives you got? Five? Six?"

Wilgus said he didn't have any. "I ain't but eight," he said. "And my name ain't Monroe, neither. It's Wilgus."

"Eight! Is that all the old you are? Why Wilgus Short, I had you figured to be up around twenty-five or thirty somewhere."

Wilgus said, "You did not. You're teasing. Here, take this old cigar back, I don't want it."

The man slammed on the brakes. Wilgus pitched forward, along with most of the tools and equipment. He would have hurt himself if he hadn't got his free hand up to catch himself on the dashboard.

4

"Don't *want* it!" the fat man exclaimed. "How come you to take it if you don't want it?"

Wilgus was too shaken to answer. Nervously he glanced at the man. Then he shoved the chainsaw around so he could sit back down as the truck began to pick up speed again. The cigar had fallen to the floor.

"Oh Lord," the fat man moaned. He wiped his face with the palm of his hand. "Oh Lordy me, why did I ever pick up this boy?" Looking at Wilgus, his lower lip drooping, he said, "You've hurt my feelings bad, boy. You really have."

And two big tears welled out of the corners of his eyes and rolled down his puffy cheeks.

Wilgus didn't have anything to say.

"You have, now," the fat man sniffed. "You really have. There I give you a nice cigar and then you tell me you don't want it anymore."

"I didn't go to hurt your feelings," said Wilgus. "But I don't really think I did."

"Listen at him," sighed the fat man. "Accusing me of telling lies. Oh Lord above, why did I ever pick up such a boy?"

"I didn't call you no liar," said Wilgus. "You're just making all that stuff up."

"You know," said the fat man. He sat up a little straighter now. "You know, Short Wilgus, I had a suspicion you was going to turn out to be mean. I didn't want to say anything about it, but I could tell, three or four

5

miles ago, I could see it in those eyes of yours. Mean, just plain m-e-a-n mean. I don't know what else to do with you but report you. Whose boy are you?"

"Glen Collier's."

"Glen Collier's what?"

"His *boy*," said Wilgus. "He's my daddy."

"You know," said the fat man. "It seems to me like I've heard of Glen Collier. Ain't he that fishing worm salesman from over on Leatherwood?"

Wilgus didn't have anything to say. He refused to even look at the man. They were passing familiar places now, within a mile or two of his house, and Wilgus stared out the window, wishing he was already home.

"If he don't sell fishing worms, what *does* he do? Talk to me now, Short Wilgus, let's get all this said while we've got the chance."

"Daddy loads coal for the Harlowe brothers when there's work."

"And your mommy? How does he treat your mommy?"

"Daddy's real good to us," said Wilgus.

"Well that ain't the way I heard it," said the fat man, and he clucked his tongue and shook his head knowingly.

"What do you mean?" Wilgus asked.

"Somebody told me your daddy drunk whiskey, played all his money away on cards, laid out on the weekends and that when he *would* come home. . . ."

"That's not so. My daddy's good."

"How often does he beat your mommy up?"

6

"My daddy's *good*."

"That ain't the way I heard it," said the fat man. "I heard he beat on you and was too sorry to work and that him and your mommy fit one another all the time, that they just fit and throwed things and rassled all over the floor. And that she went out with boy friends and he went out with girl friends and left you at the house all by yourself without anything to eat and no coal for the stove. Now me, I don't blame you for hating a man like that. If *my* daddy had ever treated me like that. . . ."

"None of that's so!" Wilgus cried. "I *like* my mommy and I *like* my daddy, and that's the last thing I'm going to say. And I'm going to tell him on you too if you don't hush."

"But *why*, Wilgus? *Why* do you like them? That's the point?"

"Because I just do," said Wilgus. "They're my mommy and daddy ain't they?"

"I don't know," said the fat man. "Are they?"

He broke into such violent laughter then the truck started swerving back and forth across the road. Great tears rolled down his puffy cheeks. His eyes seemed to roll back inside his head as he tossed his head, laughing.

"Oh me," he groaned. "Oh Lordy me, what a boy this is."

But gradually the fat man's laughter became a fit of hoarse coughing. He rocked back and forth, clutching the steering wheel with both hands, sucking for air, turning red in the face from the effort. "Hit me on the back, boy, hit me on the back. Hit me on the back, I'm dying."

Wilgus watched him anxiously, trying to understand what he was supposed to do.

"Hit me on the back, Short Wilgus. Quick!"

"Do you really want me to?" Wilgus yelled above the noise.

"Oh Lord yes, hit me, hit me, I'm dying."

Wilgus wanted to hit him. He wanted very much to hit the fat man, hard, in the face, on the head. He wanted to pick up one of the heavy wrenches from the floor and hit him hard enough to kill him. He slapped him once on his thick neck. He made a fist and struck him on his enormous back, then again and again. He hit him on the shoulder and along the neck. With both hands he beat the fat man with all his might, pounding him about the neck and back and shoulders.

Wilgus was crying now.

"Whoa! Whoa!" someone shouted into the truck. "Whoa there tiger, take it easy."

The voice belonged to Wilgus' father. In a sudden cloud of dust the truck had veered off the highway onto the narrow dirt lane that led to Wilgus' house. They'd driven right into the yard and stopped at the edge of the coal pile, where his father stood with a bucket in his hand, grinning.

"He's a pure-god wildcat, this 'un is," the fat man said as he clambered out of the truck to shake Glen's hand. "You've raised you a tough 'un there now Glen, I declare you have."

Laughing, Wilgus' father glanced into the truck where his son sat wiping his eyes. He was a lanky, thin-muscled man with a miner's cap on, and no shirt. The galluses of his faded overalls lay against his bare, pale miner's skin.

Wilgus' father looked strange without a shirt on. It was strange to see him in the daytime without coal dust on his face. He was clean and shaved, and he'd got a haircut somewhere that day. His father looked so different that in some ways Wilgus didn't recognize him. The light refracting off the windshield seemed to curve him. It even made his words, his voice, sound curved.

"Aye god, don't I know it," Glen said, shaking his head and smiling proudly. "You've got to watch out for that Wilgus. He'll beat your ears off if you ain't careful."

"He like to beat me to pieces," said the fat man. "All I did was allow what a scoundrel you are and *pow*, he lit in on me till I thought I was a goner."

"He's my defender, that boy is," said Glen.

And Glen took his old friend Monroe Short by the arm and led him away, talking and laughing about the old days.

Wilgus sat in the truck, watching them.

Then he jumped out and ran across the dusty yard to the house, where his mother was.

THE FAVOR

Wilgus thought his grandfather seemed a whole lot slower today than usual. The old man shuffled along with his head bowed down, looking tired and a little angry. Wilgus had heard him trading sharp words with his grandmother earlier in the day. But that was a common enough thing lately. There was something about his grandfather now that was altogether uncommon, something in his tone that was as foreign to the man as all those brand-new clothes. Ordinarily he spoke in such a soft and gentle manner it was a comfort to hear his voice. But just now when he said, "Come with me to the field, Wilgus, a section of fence is down," his voice had been as heavy and nervous as it was in church when Brother Ellis called on him to pray.

And his clothes. From head to toe his grandfather had on brand-new clothes. New hat, new shoes, khaki pants with blue suspenders and a new white shirt he wore open at the collar, the sleeves rolled up to his elbows. Sometimes his grandfather dressed like that when he went to the polls to vote. But here he was, a hammer in one hand and a sack of nails in the other, sweating already, setting out in the heat of the afternoon to do a job of work. It was all so odd the normally talkative boy followed the old man to the barn without a word.

They stopped at the barn long enough to pick up a roll of wire. Then, Wilgus carrying one end, his grandfather carrying the other, side by side they walked out beyond the garden, past his grandmother's grape arbor and patch of strawberries, walked on without speaking till they rounded the bend of the hill.

But as soon as the house was out of sight behind them, the grandfather said, "Hold up a minute, Wilgus, let's rest ourselves." And he laid the wire and the hammer and nails on the ground. The old man looked all around, at the trees up the hill a ways from where they stood, then out across the narrow valley that dropped away below. He took out his handkerchief and wiped his forehead and his neck. He put the handkerchief back in his pocket, and rearranged his hat. Then he looked at his grandson and in a nervous voice confessed he hadn't brought him out to fix a fence at all.

Wilgus asked him what they'd come for, then.

"I need you to do me a favor," said the grandfather.

And he went on to tell the boy what was on his mind.

He was leaving home, he said. Going away for good. Leaving the farm, divorcing his wife, leaving Kentucky altogether, to go and live his life in another place. He wanted Wilgus to take that news to his grandma, and take some money to her he'd drawn out of the bank that morning. He reached into his pocket and brought out a roll of bills.

"Now give this to her, Wilgus. Tell her to stretch it, 'cause I've got the rest of the cash and gone with it. Oh, now, she'll scream and carry on, you might as well expect it. But it's just noise. I've stood it forty years nearly, you can stand it a minute or two. She's getting the place here. It's got a life of work in it, I reckon it ought to equal the dollars I'm taking. Anyhow it's her'n. I don't bear no grudges, tell her. She might. That's her privilege. But all my life, back and forth, pillar to post, tell her . . ." The old man's voice trailed away then and for a moment he was silent. "Don't tell her nothing," he went on. "Just give this to her and don't tell her nothing except I'm gone."

And he counted out a hundred dollars in Wilgus' hand.

But he didn't put his roll of bills back into his pocket right away. He stood there looking thoughtfully at all the fives and tens and twenties that he held. Sucking his teeth, shaking his head dubiously, he finally peeled off another twenty and put it in the boy's hand.

"If you'll take that to your Grandma, it'll be a big help to me."

Wilgus looked at the money in his hand. "But ain't you never coming home no more?" he asked.

The grandfather quit fidgeting and for the first time that afternoon he grinned and spoke in a voice that sounded like himself. "Oh," he said. "I expect I'll see *you* again one of these days."

"But where are you going to live?"

"Well," said the grandfather. "I'm going to Floyd County for a spell. Then on over to Virginia, like as not. But I'd rather you didn't mention that to your grandma. You can keep a secret, can't you?"

Wilgus mumbled that he could. He started to ask another question, there was a lot he wanted to find out about, and to say. But somehow he couldn't get enough of it straight in his mind to form a sentence. And his grandfather seemed about out of words himself. He told Wilgus to be a good boy. Wilgus said he would. They shook hands. Then abruptly the grandfather turned and walked away, angling downhill toward the valley where the railroad was.

Wilgus took off running hard the other way.

Later, when he had his breath again, and a sense of where he was, lying on his back on the cool flat rock beside the pasture creek, Wilgus felt light in the head. It was as if he had gone to sleep when he shook hands with his grandfather, and dreamed his frantic run through trees and across a wide, steep field. Dreamed two cows had stopped their grazing to watch him running by. Dreamed his tears, dreamed the hot constriction in his chest. At one point Wilgus' lungs had felt so hot he wondered if people everywhere weren't dying because they couldn't breathe. It all might as well have been a dream, for it was fading now as he rested quietly on the rock. He felt his breathing slowly falling back to normal. He felt his heart regain its calm and easy rhythm. All along his spine, the purest sense of ease that he had ever known was flowing smoothly.

Lying there, feeling the rock beneath him, hearing the water flowing past his head while overhead the leaves of the pawpaw trees brushed and flapped together, Wilgus felt something fresh inside him. Something was trying to occur to him. What was it? He didn't know. It was a feeling, a sense, that somehow this was it: everything he cared about was now at stake. In his hands. Up to him.

The question was whether or not he was up to it.

The glory was that he believed he was.

Wilgus was amazed that such a feeling was growing inside him. Suddenly his own mind awed him, he felt so powerful and so wise. All he had to do was simply lie there and it would happen. If he moved, if he stirred in the slightest, his idea would disappear before it had fully formed, and more loss than he could stand would be upon him. But if he lay still, if for once in his life he could resist his impulse to talk and do, if he could be quiet in this rare moment and give this force inside him room to grow, then all he cared about, all the things and people that he knew would be delivered, safe, and life could then go on and on and on.

Silently, now. Still.

Wilgus felt the sweat and tears drying on his skin. The creek was in slow motion just beneath his rock. Overhead the leaves of the pawpaw trees moved and rustled. Somewhere far away a solitary crow was cawing.

As long as Grandma doesn't know that Grandad's gone, it hasn't happened yet.

Wilgus sat up straight and thought: I could even sketch it if I wanted to. It would be a drawing of his grandfather getting mad and throwing something at his grandmother, a rock, a curse, a lightning bolt. And there Wilgus was, catching the bolt in his bare hands, taking the awful shock into his own body before it could strike and wound her.

With a whoop Wilgus jumped down off his rock, stripped off all his clothes and in celebration plunged into the shallow creek.

The water only came up to his knees, but by lying down and pretending, it was as good as Buckhorn Lake to him. Wilgus ducked his head and rolled and tumbled and came up spouting and splashing joyfully. His thrashing made the water muddy but when he lay still again and again grew thoughtful, the mud settled and the stream ran clear enough to drink.

As long as Grandma doesn't know, it hasn't happened yet. She can't know if I don't tell her, and if I don't tell her she can never know.

Oh, she'll know he's *gone* all right. No preventing that. If Grandad wasn't going to live at the homeplace anymore she'd certainly know he was gone. But she didn't have to know why he was gone, what the circumstances of his leaving were. Grandad was gone, that's all. Disappeared. A mystery.

And Wilgus would become a mystery too. Oh yes. He would have to leave too, now. For his grandma's sake. To save her from the terrible thing he knew. It was a painful thing to think about but it had to be that way. For Wilgus knew that if he ever saw his grandma again he'd tell her all about Grandad leaving, tell her what he'd said. Maybe he'd even break down and tell her where he'd gone. She deserved better than that. She deserved to never know. It was a lonesome prospect, his grandfather over in Floyd County, Wilgus out on the road somewhere while his grandma lived all alone there in the house, sad old woman now. It would be tough on them all, but even so, even if they all were sad and lonely the rest of their lives, still they'd be lonely inside a web of love. At least they would have their memories of each other to be fond of. At least there still would be the past to care about.

But as Wilgus considered it, swimming and thinking in the cold creek water, the idea of going away began to seem a little severe for the way he really felt inside. Wilgus knew he couldn't live with his grandma in a daily way anymore. But perhaps he ought to stay nearby, live in walking distance of the house, secretly look in on her from time to time, keep a watch above her, do secret things to help her get along. Some mornings she'd get up and see her garden plowed, see her fruit trees pruned, her fences mended, and she would wonder: now just who on earth did that for me?

Wilgus looked around at the creek banks then, and suddenly saw how it would be. He saw the cabin he would build, a log house with mud daubed in the cracks, set back under the pawpaw trees. On the walls were animal hides, bear and coon and deer. He looked down the creek a ways to where the channel bent. There on the little bottom was where he'd have his garden. He'd drink from the creek, of course. Just below his little pool the water ran clear and pure over moss and clean, dark stones. In season wild strawberries covered the steep slope that was the pasture, and after them the blackberries came. Along the margins of the creek wild lettuce grew, and mint, and in the fall the soft pawpaws fell to the ground, as good as bananas when you're hungry.

And what the land could not provide, hard cash would. Wilgus was out of the water now, surveying his domain. He took the money out of his pocket, counted it again. That money had been ugly to him so far, a burden that weighed him down. Now it was only wealth and Wilgus ran it through his fingers, counting it again. It occurred to him to hide it, as a safeguard. As he slipped it under a certain rock he thought of the tools and equipment he would buy, the grain and the team of mules he'd use to start his homestead with.

Once the vision was complete in his mind, Wilgus put his clothes on and went to work clearing underbrush away from where the cabin was going to be. He pulled weeds and hacked at roots for over an hour. Then instead of resting he started carrying stones for the foundation and the chimney he would build. He went down to the creek's bend and in the flat place paced off his garden, thirty feet by ten. On his way back up he foraged among the rocks for mint and watercress. Then for a while he worked on his little rock dam. He'd started it earlier in the summer but hadn't got very far. Now in half an hour he did as much work as he'd done earlier in three or four days, and he would have finished it if the sun had not gone down. But it went down, a shadow passed across the water, and then it was too cold to work in the water anymore. Wilgus put his shoes on and carried chimney stones another hour. Likely he would have kept on working till after dark if suddenly the image of his grandfather had not fallen across the water at his feet.

"What are you doing, son, building yourself a town?"

The old man's sudden presence took Wilgus' breath away. Trembling, the boy let go of the rock he was lifting and stood up.

It was him, all right. It was Grandad Collier, in the

flesh. And more him now than ever. The tension that had burdened his voice at noon was gone. And so were his dress-up clothes. It was just his grandfather now, wearing his familiar work clothes and his old hat, walking toward him, crossing the creek on the stones of Wilgus' dam.

"Well. You *have* been busy," said the grandfather, looking around the camp. "You move all that rock yourself?"

"I thought you went away."

The grandfather cleared his throat. "Well," he said. "I got as far as town. But I got to thinking about it. I figured I better come on back home for a while. See what happens. That all right with you?"

"But you said you was leaving home for good."

"Well, Wilgus. It's a long story. I'll tell it to you one of these days. What I'd rather talk about right now is my hundred dollars. You never spent it, did you? I notice you never took it to your grandma at the house."

Wilgus went to the hiding place and got the money.

"It's a hundred and twenty," he said.

"I tell you what," said his grandfather. "Let's call it an even hundred and ten. I'd like to give you ten dollars, for a present."

"I don't want no present."

"For wages, then. It looks to me like you've put in a pretty hard day, clearing this ground, moving all this rock around."

"Oh," said the boy. "I just been playing."

"Well," said the grandfather. "You've played hard. And you've done me a real good favor. Here." And he put the ten in the boy's pocket and made him keep it.

It was nearly dark by the time they got to where they'd left the tools and wire. And by the time they got back to the barn, full night had come. Wilgus stood outside while his grandfather went in the barn to put the tools away. Across the dark back yard he saw the lighted windows of the house. There in the kitchen was his grandmother, standing by the stove. *Grandma*, Wilgus thought. *There she is.* And when his grandfather came out of the barn and the two of them started walking together toward the house he thought: *Grandad. Here he is.* And there it was again: a feeling, deep inside, trying to occur, an idea that Wilgus would be a long time knowing. But that was okay. Let it take its time. He was a patient man. Just knowing that one day he would know was quite enough for now.

NIGHT RIDE

Delmer pulled up in front of his mother's house and blew the horn.

His nephew Wilgus came running out the back door carrying his jacket in his hand.

The boy's grandmother chased him through the back door and across the porch yelling, "Wilgus! Wilgus! You listen to me!"

But by the time she reached the steps the boy was already climbing into his uncle's car.

"You be careful with that child!" she yelled to Delmer.

"See you later!" Delmer yelled back laughing.

The gravel flew as he wheeled his Ford around and scratched off down the hill toward the county road.

But there was a stop Delmer had to make before

they left the Trace Fork road and struck the highway. In front of his cousin Vernon's house near the mouth of the creek Delmer slammed on the brakes and jumped out of the car almost before it quit rolling. He ran across Vernon's front yard and disappeared into his house, then came double-timing back again before Wilgus had time to tune the car radio.

"Here you go," said Delmer as he handed Wilgus a paper bag containing two sixpacks of ice cold bootleg beer. "Set this on the floor." Laughing rather madly, Delmer got in behind the wheel. As he set the car in motion again he took a pint of whiskey out of his pocket and told Wilgus to put it in the glove compartment.

Wilgus had to shift Delmer's pistol and ammunition and some other junk around to make room for the bottle. In the process a package of Trojan rubbers fell out on the floor. Wilgus picked them up and put them back in the compartment.

"Open me a beer, Wilgus," said Delmer as he shifted into high gear and reached to tune the radio better. It had been screeching and squawking since Wilgus turned it on. Delmer searched the dial while Wilgus put two holes in a beer can with a church key he found in the glove compartment. As Mac Wiseman sang "I Wonder How the Old Folks Are at Home," Wilgus handed the beer to his uncle. Delmer took a deep drink, then handed the can back to Wilgus.

Wilgus was only thirteen but he knew about beer. He'd been sipping it from other people's bottles as long as he could remember and he thought it was fine stuff indeed. Wilgus had never actually had his own full can to drink all by himself before. But when he took this sip he suddenly realized it was time. For there he was, cruising along the highway, leaning hard around the curves, heading off with his uncle with two six packs of beer and Mac Wiseman singing on the radio. If this wasn't the time for him to have his own beer there would never be one. Wilgus handed Delmer's beer can back, opened one for himself, then settled back into the corner of the suicide seat to drink and watch the world flash by.

The Finley County line flashed by. And a bunch of people hanging around in front of Cottrell's store. Three boys playing basketball on a dirt court in a school yard flashed by, and two other old boys sitting on the rail of the bridge that crossed Columbus Creek whizzed by too. They lifted their hands in greeting and Wilgus, grinning broadly, returned their wave with the hand that held the beer.

Delmer was driving so fast, every time they hit a sudden dip in the road Wilgus' stomach rose up toward his heart and thrilled him through and through. They hit one dip that felt so good Delmer slammed on the brakes, backed up and took it again even faster. Wilgus was just then finishing his first beer, and as it flowed through his blood

25

and brain, the only thing he could think to do to express his feeling was stick his head out the window and yell *wheeee!*

Delmer laughed and told the boy to hand him another beer. He downed a third of it in one gulp, then told Wilgus to get the pistol out, he felt like shooting awhile. Wilgus got the heavy .38 out of the glove compartment and handed it to Delmer.

"Steer this thing," said Delmer, letting go of the wheel without slowing down in the slightest. Wilgus took the wheel as his uncle leaned out the window and began to fire. Shooting left-handed, Delmer drilled two roadsigns. Then he pointed the gun in the air and fired off the remaining rounds. Delmer handed Wilgus the pistol and told him to reload it.

Wilgus knew about guns, too. His father had given him a single-shot .22 the year before he died. And Delmer, and Delmer's brother Junior, let him shoot their pistols from time to time. The last Fourth of July when Junior had come down from Cincinnati for the three-day weekend, they had all been out behind the barn at the homeplace, blazing away with their pistols at the salt block on the stump, and Wilgus had blown one whole corner off with his first shot. The .38 was heavy in Wilgus' hands but he reloaded it smoothly and put it back in the glove compartment. Then he opened himself a second beer and settled back into his corner again.

People were driving with their parking lights on now,

and at the Dwarf junction Delmer turned his on too. There was still light in the sky but the valley was filling up with shadows. As they rolled along Route 80 toward Hindman, Wilgus looked out the window at the people still working in their gardens in front of their homes along Troublesome Creek. They were old people mostly, walking in the rows, dusting the plants, or digging in the balks with hoes. One old man was leading a mule up a path toward a log barn. Another man was walking across a swinging bridge carrying a load of groceries in a box on his shoulder. All the people still working after sundown made Wilgus think about his grandparents, who had probably worked through the evening in the garden back at the homeplace. If Wilgus had been at home he would have worked with them. He would have gone to the pasture to drive the old cow in for his grandfather to milk. He would have carried coal and kindling into the kitchen for the morning cooking fire. The picture in his mind of his grandmother and grandfather working alone in the last hours of daylight made Wilgus feel a little sad. But he was too excited by the beer and the gunshots and the speed and swaying motion of the car to fall to brooding. Coming up behind an old slow Plymouth, Delmer nearly touched its rear bumper with his front one at sixty miles an hour. Then, with a curve only a few hundred feet ahead, Delmer pulled out into the other lane and roared around the Plymouth, pulling back into the right-hand lane just in time to miss a Studebaker coming toward them around

27

the curve. When they had survived the curve upright and settled into steady cruising again, Delmer leaned forward, patted the dashboard and said, "The forty Ford's the finest car ever made."

Wilgus opened another beer for his uncle. Once they had passed through the town of Hindman and headed out through Carr Fork toward Cody over on Route 15, Wilgus opened a third one for himself. He settled into his seat ready to cruise on another half hour before he budged again. But then without announcement, Delmer slowed to thirty, then twenty, and then he brought the Ford to a stop in front of a little dwelling house whose front yard nearly touched the highway.

"You wait here," said Delmer as he turned the motor off and opened the door to get out. "I've got to go in here and see a man about a dog."

"Take your time," said Wilgus, hoisting his beer aloft in a toast to the sudden stop. He watched as Delmer stood ouside the car stuffing his shirt into his trousers neatly, then smoothing his long dark hair with a pocket comb. Delmer patted his sideburns and rolled the cuffs of his pale green shirt another turn toward his elbows. Wilgus watched his uncle walk across the narrow yard and bound up the steps to the front porch of the little house.

Wilgus looked closely to see what the woman who lived there looked like. He knew it was a woman Delmer was going to see. Before Delmer could knock she opened the door and Wilgus got a glimpse of her. He couldn't tell if she was good-looking or not, but he saw enough to at least imagine that she was. She had blonde hair, and some kind of kerchief around her neck. Behind her he saw the pink wallpaper on the living room wall, and an unshaded lightbulb dangling on a cord from the ceiling. She glanced past Delmer as he walked in, and if it had been lighter outside her eyes would have met Wilgus'. But it was dark now, or very nearly so. She closed the door and a second later Wilgus saw a hand pull down the shade over the front window.

Wilgus understood that Delmer might not be coming out of the house for a good long time, and he searched around in his mind to see if he cared or not. He decided that he didn't. He decided, in fact, that he liked it, that they had stopped, that Delmer was in a strange house with a strange woman and he was outside in the car by himself with a good beer in his hand. A lovely summer evening was settling into night outside. From somewhere behind the house Wilgus heard a creek warbling in the dark. He felt the moisture thickening in the air. It came in through the car window and touched his neck and arm. In the yard was a little silver-leaf maple tree, just like the maples in the yard back at the homeplace. Their leaves flapping and flickering silver in the dark made Wilgus think about the homeplace again, about how far he was away from it now, away from his grandma and grandad.

Wilgus had lived with his grandparents most of his life so far. Their house had been his home even before his parents died. Their house was the place he was away from now. I am far away, Wilgus told himself. Far away and moving on, cruising through the night with my Uncle Delmer who is in that house by the side of the road with some strange woman, probably fucking with her by now. Wilgus knew about fucking. He'd known about it longer than anybody in his family would have dared to guess, Delmer included. He'd never personally done any, but it was in the boy's mind to try it the first chance he got. Maybe Delmer had his chance right now. Maybe that's what he and that woman were doing. The thought made the boy excited and happy and he went on drinking beer and waiting and listening to the radio.

Wilgus would have been satisfied to sit there the rest of the night like that. But about twenty minutes after he went in, Delmer came storming out of the house, cursing wildly over his shoulder at the woman who had followed him to the doorway. Wilgus got a good look at her now. She was more than good-looking. She was beautiful. He couldn't see her face because the light was behind her, but he saw her shape, he saw the fullness of her. It was the most disappointing thing in the world to see Delmer walking away from her in a cursing rage. Wilgus kept his eyes on the woman standing on the porch as Delmer got back in the car and started the motor and roared off furiously down the highway.

Delmer drove a good fifteen minutes without taking his eyes off the road. Finally he leaned across and opened the glove compartment and got the pint of whiskey out. He took a drink, then another, then replaced the bottle without offering Wilgus any. Wilgus didn't mind. There wasn't any way that whiskey could improve on what the beer was doing to his head. Wilgus sipped his beer and studied his uncle, who sat slumped against the door with one elbow hanging casually out the window. In profile he looked very much like his brother, Wilgus' father, Glen. His body was shaped the same. Except for his arms, which were thick and powerful-looking, Delmer was a lean and wiry man, not as tall as Glen, but proportioned like him. Now and then Delmer rubbed his hand across his face, lightly massaging the flesh. That was a gesture Wilgus' father had made a lot too. Delmer looked weary and sad and angry now as Wilgus studied him in the glow of the dashboard lights. Wilgus tried to think of something to say. But there wasn't anything to say, so the boy leaned his head out the window and breathed the cool night air as Delmer ignored the stop sign at the village of Cody and turned onto Route Fifteen, headed south.

Rolling on into Letcher County now, going up old Garner Mountain, they came upon a pickup going so slow Delmer had to slow down quick to keep from hitting it. Blowing his horn and cursing, he pulled into the left lane to pass. He got around the pickup okay but before he could get back into the right lane he came to a curve, and a car coming downhill from the other direction had to take the shoulder to keep from hitting Delmer's Ford.

The car was full of men and boys about as drunk as Delmer and Wilgus were, and as they passed they blew their horn wildly and filled the night with angry shouts and curses. Delmer slowed and reached for his pistol in case those guys wanted to stop and fight about it. But they didn't. They were on their way to Vicco to get more booze and they kept rolling on down Garner the way Delmer and Wilgus had just come, finally disappearing into the night.

"Let's take a piss-break," Delmer said, and he eased the car off the road on a wide place at the inside of a curve.

As they stood by the roadside peeing, Delmer and Wilgus stared up at the stars which were popping out all over heaven by now. It was a clear night without much moon. The Milky Way would be brilliant in a couple of hours. As he zipped his pants Delmer said, "Sure is a nice night out, ain't it?"

Wilgus agreed that it was. To celebrate the night and their pleasant pause by the roadside, Delmer fired off a few rounds from his .38. He shot a beer can lying in a ditch. He fired a couple of rounds through the windshield of an old abandoned car lying on its side among some trees down the bank from the road. Then he handed the pistol to Wilgus and told him to empty the chamber. Grinning, giggling a little, weaving a little unsteadily on his feet, Wilgus aimed at the western horizon where there was still just the faintest trace of light in the sky, and pulled the trigger three times. Each shot caused the pistol to buck in his hand and throw his arm head-high. The shock sent thrills down Wilgus' spine that stayed with him as they got back in the car.

"By god," Delmer laughed. "This is the wild side of life ain't it Wilgus?"

Wilgus just grinned and opened them another beer.

At Sawdust Junction on the south side of Garner Mountain Delmer turned right onto Kentucky 7 and drove through the sleeping communities of Jeremiah, Letcher and Blackey, then on through Ulvah and Cornettsville. At Cornettsville Delmer turned onto a gravel road that led toward Leatherwood, Gordon and the Harlan County line a few miles on.

"Place up here I want to show you," Delmer said, swigging his beer.

Delmer stopped the car in front of a hillside that was on fire. It wasn't really a hillside burning. It was a slagheap big as a hill, steaming all over, and on fire in a hundred different places. Wilgus had seen plenty of slate dumps burning before, but he'd never seen one this big. The great mound of burning slag was the refuse of several decades from one of the biggest industrial mines in Kentucky, and the flames on it lit the entire night with a pale orange glow. The fires were not bright enough to read by but they were plenty bright for Wilgus and Delmer to see each other's faces, and they grinned drunkenly and happily as they stood beside the car.

Carrying their beer, they walked onto the heap a ways

and stood near one of the small patches of fire. Before long they felt the heat through their shoes and they had to back up some. After a long time of silent looking Delmer said, "Me and your Dad put some of the slate on this pile."

"*This* pile?" said Wilgus.

Delmer nodded. He sipped his beer and wiped his mouth with the back of his hand. Then he took a few steps backward and sat down in the weeds by the roadside, and Wilgus sat down beside him.

"Glen worked at Blue Diamond four years, before you was born. Then I come and worked a while. First job for wages I ever had. I didn't stay long. The war come. But the slate we dug went on that very pile yonder. It was on fire then and there it is, still yet burning. That's something to think about."

Wilgus sat there thinking about it. He didn't know what he thought, exactly. It was a feeling he had as much as it was a thought. But it was powerful, all the same. The beer running through his system and the flames and sulphur fumes rising out of the earth on the night air added up to a mystery and a power greater than any Wilgus had ever felt before. The boy sat there fishing around in his mind for some words to attach to his feeling when suddenly his mind was blown away by the great thunder of Delmer's .38, blam! blam! blam! and incredible sweet thrills ran up Wilgus' spine into his dizzy spinning mind.

For the next hour, or two, or maybe even three, Delmer and Wilgus sat by the slag heap drinking and shooting the pistol at the little pools of fire winking at them in the darkness. And in the intervals between the great explosions of the gun they talked to each other in a way they never had before. They talked about their family, about the old days among the Colliers on Trace Fork. They talked about their relatives who had died. Delmer asked Wilgus if he ever thought about his father much.

"I think about him," said Wilgus.

"He sure was a good old boy," said Delmer. "He was the best one of us, that's for sure. Thing about Glen, he was smart. I mean *really* smart. I mean, he was just an old dogface in the war. And he mined coal like the rest of us. But Glen could have been anything he wanted to be if he'd had the chance. Lawyer. Doctor. Glen could have been a college professor if he'd had the chance."

Wilgus swigged his beer. "Me and him used to work crossword puzzles together."

"He could do things like that," said Delmer. "He could write the prettiest letters of anybody."

"I've still got some of his letters," said Wilgus.

"Well you keep them letters," said Delmer. "Keep 'em and read 'em again when you're older. You'll see a lot of stuff in 'em you maybe don't see right now."

Delmer shot the pistol at the slagheap, then handed the gun to Wilgus. Wilgus didn't feel like shooting it just

35

then. He opened out the cylinder, took out the bullets and empty casings, spun the cylinder a time or two, then loaded it again.

"Who was that woman?" he asked.

An hour ago Wilgus would have been afraid to mention the woman to his uncle. But now the question popped out easily and naturally, taking its place in the intimacy of the moment alongside everything else they'd talked about. And Delmer answered the question as easily and naturally as Wilgus had asked it.

"Woman I've been seeing," he said. "Pauline's her name."

"She's pretty," said Wilgus.

Delmer nodded and stared at the fires. "She's a real good woman. Me and her might get married one of these days."

"Married! No kidding?"

Delmer chuckled. "Yeah. We didn't act like it much a while ago though, did we?" And he laughed and took a drink of whiskey and chased it down with beer. When he'd wiped his mouth Delmer said in a more serious tone, "I've tried to tell her I'm a son of a bitch but she won't listen."

"You're not a son of a bitch."

"Yes I am too," said Delmer. And he took the pistol from Wilgus and fired six rounds rapidly at the nearest patch of flame.

"Let's go over to the car, listen to the radio awhile," he said.

They found a late-night Nashville station playing nigger-music that was just right for the mood Wilgus and Delmer had established for themselves. The music was one more thing that reminded Wilgus of his grandparents, who were sleeping now back at the homeplace. Some nights, after the old folks had gone to bed, Wilgus would get under the covers with his radio and listen to the distant stations, Cincinnati and Louisville, Chicago and Fort Wayne, and sometimes when conditions were right, even Del Rio, Texas. But his favorite station was WLAC out of Nashville, because of the rhythm and blues they played. Right now in the car Johnny Ace was singing "Pledging My Love." Wilgus had listened to that very song not two nights ago. Hearing it now made him think about his grandparents, asleep in bed at the homeplace, except for maybe his grandmother who tended to lie awake when she was expecting people to come into her house late in the night. Probably she was lying awake right now, waiting for him and Delmer to get home, worrying about them, wondering where they were.

Well, where were they? Goddamn, who knew? Way off in Perry County somewhere, close to the Harlan County line. When you got close to Harlan County you were close to the Virginia line. And when you were in Virginia, you were in a state that ended at the ocean. Think of that.

37

The Atlantic Ocean, just on beyond those hills there.

For that matter, think of the ocean in this very valley here, a million years ago. That's what they'd said in school. These very hills used to be underneath the ocean. These very valleys used to be swamps. And in the swamps grew ferns and flowers and the ferns and flowers turned into coal and then my daddy dug that coal. Dug it right out of these hills here. Dumped the gob on that very pile there, twenty years ago. And it was on fire then and it's on fire now and maybe it'll burn forever, who knows?

Wilgus started to say something to Delmer about the ocean and the ferns and coal. But when he turned to speak, he found his uncle slumped over on the seat, passed out. The pint bottle lay on the floor. Wilgus picked it up and held it to the light of the burning hill. There was one small drink left in it. Wilgus tipped the bottle up and swallowed. The whiskey burned his throat like sulphur smoke but he liked it. He liked the beer he'd had that evening. He liked the night they'd driven through. He liked their ride and he liked their talk. He liked Delmer. Wilgus loved old Delmer. He liked the slate dump, the flame and smoke, the forever on-going fire. He liked the way the whiskey ran straight to his head and cleared it, focused it, made him see exactly what he should do.

What he should do is get behind the wheel and drive the car back home. Wilgus wasn't the best driver in the world but he had confidence that he could manage it. He'd driven the Ford up and down Trace Fork a few times. And his Uncle Junior usually let him drive his Chevrolet when he came home from Cincinnati.

Wilgus could drive.

He raked the empty beer cans out onto the roadside, then put the empty pistol back in the glove compartment. He pushed and tugged at Delmer's inert body until he had room to sit behind the wheel. Wilgus forgot to let the handbrake off and the car wouldn't go at first. But then he remembered the brake and he let it off and the car wheeled in a circle on the gravel road and headed back down the valley toward Cornettsville, toward Finley County, toward Trace Fork and the homeplace, fifty some miles away.

THE FIGHT

My Grandma Collier and her daughter Jenny have been quarreling with one another as long as I can remember. After my father died and before Jenny married Russell Patch, she and Grandma more or less raised me, and their feud has been a kind of running theme throughout my life. Over the years I've seen them fight about everything from what to have for supper to whether or not Jenny ought in fact to marry Russell Patch. And when she did marry him and move away, still the fights went on through the mail and over the telephone and on Jenny's periodic visits home. I thought that after Russell died last year Jenny might mellow a little and she and Grandma would start getting along a little better. But no. If anything, they got worse. Not long ago I was home from college for the weekend and there they were, at it again.

With her hands on her hips and a hurt expression on her face Jenny was saying, "Well Mommy honey, it's no wonder Daddy says he can't breathe. There's no good air in a coal district, they can't *nobody* breathe any good around here."

"Can't breathe," Grandma scoffed. "Did that old fool tell you he can't breathe? Well God bless us all, what next? If it ain't his back it's his head and if it ain't his head it's rheumatism in his legs. Can't breathe. I say can't breathe. Keep on pettin' him and you'll have him till he's too sorry to roll over in bed."

"Oh, Mommy, Daddy is *sick*," Jenny pleaded. "Why I can tell a big difference in him just since I was home last."

"Well," said Grandma, "you younguns think you're all so smart. I'd just like to know how you think we've got along all these years without help from the likes of you."

"Mommy, I don't deny that," said Jenny. "You all have done good, I wouldn't take that away from you for the world. And I don't mean to throw off on your house either. I guess the best days of my life were spent here, a lot of them right here in this kitchen helping you can and cook and feed the family. I remember all of that and I wouldn't take anything for those old times but, well . . ." and Jenny sighed wearily and looked across the kitchen at me.

"Wilgus, you talk to her."

"Shoot," said Grandma. "Don't think you can fill Wilgus' head with trash. He goes to college, he's not going to let a foolish woman blow up an old man's aches and pains into any epidemic, now are you son?"

I laughed and shook my head. "I'm staying out of this," I said. "I know how you two are when you go to quarreling."

Grandma laughed expansively and hit the table with her fist. "Told you he was smart!"

Grandma is a large woman filled with energy for a woman her age, even if she doesn't get around very well anymore. There's a peculiar brand of meanness about her too that terrified me when I was a child but which charms and amuses and only occasionally intimidates me now. She was smiling broadly as she argued with Jenny, not angry yet but with a flush in her cheeks that meant she soon would be. As a gesture to try to show that she was relaxed and superior to the disagreement, Grandma casually picked up an apple from a bushel basket on the floor and began to eat it.

"It's not funny," Jenny frowned. "I really am worried about Daddy."

"That's just what he wants is somebody to pity and make over him," said Grandma. "If you want to know what I think, I think he's in his second childhood. Gone back to wanting attention pime blank like a four-year old."

"Oh, Mommy," Jenny sighed.

"It's the truth, I declare it is."

"You're just blind then!" Jenny declared. "Daddy is as sick again as he was Christmas and I'll make a prediction: if he doesn't get proper care soon something awful is going to happen."

"Listen at her," Grandma mocked. "You just don't know what a pretender your daddy is, is all. Oh, he's good at it, you've got to give the devil his due. That man can pout and moan and carry on till folks that didn't know better would swear that he was dying. That old rip's been sittin' on his butt in there since Thanksgiving saying oh my head, oh my back, oh this and oh that, when they ain't nary thing wrong with him that a good dose of work won't cure. Ain't that what you say, Wilgus?"

"Don't think you can fool Wilgus, Mommy. *He* knows how things are. Don't you, honey?"

Both women looked at me to see what I would say. I swallowed the last of my cornbread and dusted the crumbs off my hands. I told them I thought it was silly to argue about someone else's health.

"It's not silly when somebody's life's at stake, Wilgus," said Jenny.

"Pshht! Now listen at that. Somebody's life at stake. All I can see at stake is who's boss of this house, me or you," Grandma exclaimed. "For that's all this amounts to, you trying to come in here and take over because you think your old Mommy's gettin' a little age on her."

"Now Mommy you know that's not so," said Jenny angrily. "I don't have the least desire to boss you or this

44

house. I'm just concerned that you apparently don't give a damn what happens to my daddy, that's all. Oh, I know what you'll say. You'll say you're both getting along fine here, got plenty to eat, and that your doctor book says an airy house is the best kind for old people. Well all I can say is, a lot of good an airy house is if the air itself ain't fit to breathe."

Jenny paused to catch her breath. Then she went on, "Do you know what I've decided would be the best thing in the world for Daddy?"

"It's untellin' if you thought it up."

"What Daddy needs is to live for awhile in a different climate. I think he ought to leave this old place and come and live with me awhile. I've thought about it a lot, Mommy. You can come too if you want to. But knowing you, you'd probably rather stay here and keep the place up, maybe get Mrs. Gilley to stay with you or somebody. But Daddy really does need to get away for awhile and you ought to understand that."

Grandma laid her apple on the table and solemnly folded her hands. "That's silly talk," she said.

"It's not silly, either," Jenny said excitedly. "Why our climate is a hundred per cent better than your all's here. People come to North Carolina all the time to get well. If Daddy would come and stay with me a month or two he'd be so much better you wouldn't know him when he got back."

"I wouldn't know him all right. You'd have him so

45

spoiled they wouldn't nobody know him. You sound sillier all the time, Jenny. The thing for you to do is just hush up now and mind your own business."

"Daddy *is* my business, Mommy. And let me tell you something. He's the business of more people than just me and you, and Wilgus here. He's all his children's business, and his grandchildrens', and if I have to, Mommy, I swear I'll call every one of them up long distance and tell them I'm down here trying to save Daddy's life and you won't let me. Wilgus is my witness. When we all decide to do something for Daddy, then what you think won't count."

Jenny wiped a tear from her eye. "I've tried my best to help you all, Mommy. I have. I spend over half of what I make just so you and Daddy . . . ."

"Help! Well damn such help is what I say. Nobody's asked you for nothing, Jenny. They ain't no beggars here."

Jenny jumped to her feet and shouted, "I'm talking about my Daddy dying, Mommy! He's in there, he's *dying,* right in front of all our eyes, and I just can't stand to see it, that's all!"

Jenny's eyes glistened with tears and I thought she would break down and cry. She blinked several times and wiped the tears away, then assumed an angry, determined stance and looked hard at Grandma, who looked hard in return.

That seemed like as good a time as any for me to ease out of the kitchen and go in and talk to Grandad awhile.

Grandad was sitting up straight in his rocking chair, looking intently at the chunk of cedar he was whittling on. He had on the same old clothes he always wore, overalls and a faded work shirt, buttoned at the collar and the cuffs. He was a little thin to what he was the last time I had seen him. The shirt collar wasn't as tight against his neck, his socks had fallen down his thin ankles and were lost somewhere in his old brogan shoes. But still, there he was, looking alert and comfortable, warmed by a sluggish fire in the grate, patiently shaving curls from his chunk of cedar with the small blade of his knife. He was clean-shaven, and I could tell by the neat, horizontal line of hair along the back of his head that Grandma had been working on him with her clippers.

"Looks like you've been to the barber, Grandad," I said, drawing up a chair.

"Pulled out a sight more than she cut," he replied, looking up at me for the first time. "She can't barber any better than she can doctor."

"Looks like you've had a good doctor from somewhere, though. You look better than you did. How you feeling?"

Grandad said he had been feeling better lately, and went on with his old argument, that the only thing that kept him feeling as bad as he did was the medicine he had to take. "Hot water's all I'd take if I had my way. That's nature's remedy. But you can't tell Mother nothing."

"Jenny's trying to tell her you're not doing any good."

Grandad looked at me and grinned. "I was wonderin'

47

what all that racket was about. Get Jenny and her mother together, you're sure going to have a racket."

I told Grandad that Jenny was trying to talk Grandma into letting him go home to North Carolina with her.

Grandad grunted and shook his head. "Sometimes I think Jenny's got less sense than Mother. North Carolina. Why that old woman wouldn't let me get away from her as far as Hazard. She's got to be close enough to see what I'm up to, that woman does."

"Aw, Grandad, you know you can handle the likes of Grandma."

"Ay, Lord, Wilgus. Take a lesson from it. Don't never get old before your woman does. They're hard taskmasters once they get the upper hand."

"Does that mean you'd like to get away and live with Jenny for awhile?"

Grandad shook his head. "Now what would be the difference if I did?"

I nodded, knowing what he meant. "They're pretty much alike, aren't they?"

For an answer Grandad uncrossed his legs, placed both feet flat on the floor, then slowly leaned over toward the fire. His thin jaw muscles showed through the loose, dark skin of his old face as he worked the insides of his mouth, getting ready to spit. When he was ready he pursed his lips and let fly with a powerful stream of dark tobacco juice that landed in the fire where it hissed and steamed and finally turned to powder on a glowing lump of coal. Still leaning, Grandad cupped his hand to his chin and held it there while with his tongue he pushed the frayed wad of tobacco past his lips, into his cupped hand. He worked stray bits of the chew out one at a time until he had it all collected. Then, sucking his teeth, he flung it into the fire and sat up straight again, his mouth empty now and ready for some serious talking.

Grandad is a great talker. All you have to do to get him started is ask him to tell you about times in the hills when he was a boy. Once he starts, for as long as you care to sit and listen, he'll tell you one tale after another about the old days. I get him started every chance I get because I can't help thinking what a loss it's going to be when Grandad is gone and all the old history he represents is gone with him. I was in a mood to sit there by the fire and listen to him talk the rest of the afternoon. But he hadn't any more than got rid of his chew and settled back in his chair before the door to his room flew open and Grandma and Jenny stormed in.

"Daddy," Jenny panted, "pack you a bag. I'm taking you home with me."

"Sit right there and don't move," Grandma snapped. "This girl's gone plum crazy."

"I've got more sense right now than I ever had," Jenny said. "Come on, Daddy, you know this is the right thing to do."

"Now, Jenny," I said.

"Don't now-Jenny me, Wilgus Collier. I'm serious.

Don't tell me that you of all people can stand there and not see that my daddy's a sick man, in need of care."

"I didn't say he wasn't sick. Of course he's sick."

"Pshht! Now listen at that," Grandma interrupted. "Sick. What has the old man been tellin' you, boy, how mistreated he is? Huh? That'd be about like him." She turned to look Grandad in the face. "How about it, old pooter? Is that right? Did you whine and cry to your grandboy here like you do to everybody else?"

"Grandma, he didn't whine to anybody. Now why don't you all calm down?"

"I'll be glad to calm down," said Jenny. "And while I'm at it I'll just get my daddy and go. Come on, honey," and Jenny took a step toward Grandad.

"You come back here!" Grandma yelled, and she grabbed her daughter by the arm and spun her around. As she turned, Jenny screamed and closed her eyes and swung a big haymaker at Grandma. She only hit her on the shoulder but Grandma made a face like she was half-killed. Without a word Grandma lunged past me with both hands open, reaching for Jenny's hair. Jenny raised her own hands and the women collided heavily, twisted their hands into each other's hair and began to pull and squeal and stumble in an awkward dance around the room. As I moved in to try to separate them, Grandma backed into the coal bucket and lost her balance. Letting go of Jenny's hair to try to catch herself, she stumbled over backwards and fell harshly to the floor, sending a tremor through the entire house.

Except for the ticking of Grandad's alarm clock and the slow hiss of the fire, suddenly Grandad's room was totally quiet. Jenny stood over Grandma, a look of horror on her face. Grandma didn't move. She lay there in a heap across the spilled and scattered coal, not even breathing that I could see. I was about to wonder if she was dead when, finally, her old legs stirred. Slowly they straightened and came together, ladylike. Then her arms moved, and her shoulders, as she began to lift herself, slowly pushing up her great body until she could lean on one elbow. With her free hand she pulled her dress down to cover her knees. But that seemed to tire her and for a few seconds she was still again. The color had gone from her face. Tears were in her eyes. She looked a little afraid, not knowing herself if she was hurt. But as the seconds ticked loudly off Grandma continued to come around until her color and her wind came back and she looked more indignant than damaged, more ruffled and angry now than actually hurt.

"Help her up!" Grandad commanded.

"Just leave me alone," Grandma sighed. "Just leave me alone."

"She's half-killed you!" Grandad said. He was angry and excited, sitting on the edge of his chair. Jenny turned to speak to him, but Grandad looked back at her so fiercely she burst into tears and ran out of the room.

51

I tried to talk her out of it but Jenny insisted on leaving that afternoon. The last bus from Blaine that would connect with the south-bound buses from Hazard had already run, so when I saw that she was determined to go I agreed to drive her to Harlan County, across Black Mountain to Big Stone, where she could catch the evening Tri-State to Bristol.

Jenny was still crying as we pulled away from the house. She continued to cry as we drove through Lynch and started to wind up the Big Black.

I was keyed up myself, wanting to talk. But I didn't want to impose a conversation on Jenny till she felt more like talking herself. I'd never seen her that upset before and I felt very protective toward her. She cried forlornly while I paid attention to the road. At the top of Black Mountain, without really planning to, I pulled off the road and stopped where some trees had been trimmed to open up the view that stretched away below us to the south. On a clear day you can see for miles from Black Mountain, across the tip of Southwest Virginia, into Tennessee. It was about five in the afternoon by then. Up where we were there was plenty of daylight left, but in the enormous valley below, Black Mountain's shadow was spreading rapidly across the rows of smaller hills, and here and there patches of evening mist were beginning to form and rise. Jenny gazed into the distance, and as she did, for the first time that day I had the feeling she was relaxing a little. The flesh around her mouth loosened, and she looked instantly younger for it. Her breathing became slow and even. She made fewer nervous motions with her hands.

When I put the car in gear and started on down the mountain, Jenny rearranged herself on the seat and looked at me.

"Wilgus, do you know what I've decided, just since we've been riding along here?"

"What's that, Jenny?"

"I've decided to quit worrying about people. I've decided to just let people alone from now on, let 'em get along any way they can, and start paying attention to my own life for a change. It seems like, all my life, all I've done is worry about somebody besides myself, trying to do things for people whether they wanted me to or not. And it's never occurred to me that some people might resent that. I guess that just shows how crazy I really am."

I told Jenny she wasn't crazy, but she didn't pay any attention to me.

"From now on, I'm just going to live my own life like I want to. I'm going to go back to my house and do just what I please and not worry about another living soul. Why, since Russell died, I bet I haven't spent as much as two dollars to have my hair done. And my house, Lord, it's about to fall down I've neglected it so. Of course, it's just me there by myself now. I never have felt it was worthwhile fixing up a place just for one. But Daddy won't ever leave Kentucky. Mommy won't either. It was foolish of me to mention it. So I'm going to quit worrying about Daddy now. I am. If he dies he'll just have to die, that's all. Don't you think that's the attitude to have, Wilgus? Just let everybody do what he wants to do? Ah, me," she sighed. "I think I really must be crazy."

"Shoot, Jenny, you've got more sense than anybody I know."

We were off the mountain now and driving along the valley at its base. It was cool there in the shadow of the Black and Jenny rolled her window up. She seemed to have run out of words again. She was looking out her window, deep in thought.

By the time we got to Big Stone where Jenny would catch her bus, my mind was running over with things I wanted to say. I wanted to tell Jenny that she didn't really have a choice in her feelings about her old mother and father. That choice had been made for her by who she was and things that had gone before. You're not crazy, I wanted to say. You're just lonely now. Without Grandma and Grandad to give you a reason to feel necessary, there wouldn't be anybody.

I didn't say that to Jenny, of course. But I did manage to kid her a little as we parked in front of the bus station. "Aw," I said. "You'll be back. Month or two go by, you and Grandma both'll be needing to get together so you can fight some more."

Jenny laughed. "I hope it ain't another fist fight."

As she was about to get on the bus she kissed me on the

54

cheek and said, "When I do come home again, I hope you're there too."

"I hope I am too," I said.

"Bye, honey."

"Bye, Jenny."

She waved at me through the window as the bus drove away.

THE TAIL-END OF
YESTERDAY

Evelyn had built a fire in the old coal stove to heat hot water and warm the kitchen, and she'd made the coffee on it.

"In fact," she said, "I think I'll just cook the whole breakfast on this old thing. That'll be fun. A big breakfast, over a natural fire. Don't you think so, Wilgus? I mean, breakfast, over a fire. There's just something about it, when there's work to get done, or trouble. Seems like the day just starts out better somehow."

"I'll settle for a good double martini myself," Aunt Jenny said. Still wearing her pajamas, she scurried in from the living room where she'd been sleeping and huddled next to the stove. "Brrr! What time is it, anyway, midnight?"

Evelyn told Jenny it was five-thirty. Then, to me, she

said, "Wilgus honey, we don't have any juice but here's oranges, and a Pepsi-Cola."

"What time did you get home, honey?" asked Jenny. "You look worn out."

"Just now. No thanks, Evelyn. This coffee's fine."

And it was too. I took a sip, took another, then slouched deep into my chair and for a moment closed my eyes.

"Well honey if you want anything special you just ask for it," said Evelyn. She patted my knee and smiled. "We're going to take care of you if we don't do anything else, aren't we Jenny? Jenny, this child had to stay awake all night long. Said Daddy didn't sleep a wink. Said he was out of his head talking the awfullest old crazy stuff that ever was."

"No, now, Evelyn, I didn't say it was awful."

"Oh Lord," Jenny moaned. She turned away from the stove and looked at me anxiously. Her arms hung loosely at her sides. Tears came into her eyes and I thought she was going to cry again. But instead she took a quick, nervous breath and asked me what I meant about Grandad being out of his head.

"Aw, Jenny, I don't know. He just talked. Made up crazy sayings. Phrases. He might have known a little of what he was saying, but you couldn't tell. But it wasn't awful, don't get that idea. Some of it was sort of funny, actually."

"But he's worse," said Jenny.

58

"He sounds a lot worse to me," said Evelyn.

I started to say there just wasn't any way to make any conclusions about Grandad's condition. But just then Grandma yelled, "Hush up in there!" and she pounded on her bedroom wall with her cane. "Hush up till I get there, I want to hear it!"

"Okay Mommy!" Evelyn yelled.

"But didn't Daddy sleep at *all?*" asked Jenny. "Not even a few minutes?"

"*I told you to wait!*"

Grandma stood in the doorway, looking at the three of us. Her voice was gruff and low when she said good morning. Evelyn and I said good morning, but Jenny turned away and lit a cigarette. When she shook the match out and blew a thick puff of smoke toward the ceiling Grandma looked at her meanly but she didn't say anything. Leaning heavily on her cane, bracing her free hand first on the cabinet, then the corner of the table and, coming around behind me, leaning on the chairs one by one, she made her way across the kitchen floor. Sighing, she sank heavily into the chair next to mine. Slowly she worked her ponderous old legs under the table. When at last she was established she squinted at me, grinned, and patted me affectionately on my arm.

"Well Mister Nurse-man, did old Pooter keep you up all night or what? You look like you've had a hard go-round to me."

"Mommy, Wilgus said Daddy was out of his head all night long! Said he didn't know a thing, said he just laid there talking and raving and carrying on."

"Oh, Evelyn, that's not what I said at all."

Grandma looked at me grimly. "Well," she muttered. "They've stuffed him full of old drugs, then."

"No, now, Grandma. Evelyn's got it all wrong. I didn't say...."

"I knowed they'd do it. Put old stuff in him, just make him worse so they could run up a big hospital bill on us. I wish I hadn't of took him down there now. I'm half a mind to go get him, bring him home."

"Grandma, don't jump to conclusions. Half of Grandad's trouble is he can't take medicine. They haven't given him a thing yet."

"Well they've done *something* to him, if he's out of his head. Why yesterday that man had all kinds of sense. Told me he didn't belong in no hospital. He looked me in the eye, just sensible as you please, said you old thing you, what are you doing this to me for, putting me in such a place? Well, I tried to tell him. Said now Pap, you're a sick man whether you realize it or not. You need to be here. But you know how he is. He r'ared right up and looked me in the eye and said now Mother, I ain't a-staying here. You'll see. I'll stay this one night if Wilgus'll stay with me. But tomorrow I'm coming home. You'll see."

Grandma burst out laughing. "You know," she went on. "It wouldn't surprise me a bit to look out after while

60

and see the old feller coming home. Tripping right down that highway in his nightgown, he wouldn't care. Once he gets burnt out with something. Cooped up. Old hospital. What are they feeding him, Wilgus? Bread and water?"

"I want to know what the doctor said," Jenny broke in.

But Grandma ignored her. Laughing, she said, "Why I bet Pap won't touch their old food. I bet he's said no to their soup and crackers, I bet he's laying down there dreaming about my good cornbread."

"Or cooked apples," said Evelyn. "Daddy loves cooked fruit better than anything. Wilgus honey, if we was to fix him some here at the house, do you reckon they'd let him have them?"

"I want to know what the doctor said."

Before I could answer Jenny, Uncle Delmer burst into the kitchen through the back door yelling, "What is this, a convention?" Slamming the door behind him, he walked over to the coal stove and held his hands above it. Uncle Delmer's not a heavy man but he strode into the kitchen like one, and for the first time since I'd come home from the hospital I found myself smiling. After he'd warmed his hands he crossed the kitchen and kissed Grandma on the cheek. He gave Evelyn's hair a playful tug, then turned suddenly and grabbed Jenny, forced a hug on her, told her to wipe the frown off her face and sweeten up some. Finally he took a seat at the table across from me and said, "What I can't figure out is whether this is the start of

61

today or the tail-end of yesterday. You all look to me like you've been up all night."

"Wilgus is the one," said Evelyn. "He didn't get any sleep at all."

"Out carousing I reckon," said Delmer, winking at me.

"You leave him alone!" Grandma commanded. "Wilgus has worked harder for Pap than the rest of us put together. And from the sound of it, you're not going to have any easy day with him yourself. Said Pap's lost his mind. Turned so mean on the hospital can't nobody do a thing with him."

"Oh, Grandma! I didn't say any such a thing."

"Said they filled him so full of old drugs he went plum crazy."

"No! Grandma! I didn't say that! That's his problem, he can't take drugs."

"How do you want your eggs, Wilgus, scrambled or over easy?"

"Anyway," Grandma said to Delmer. "You've got your work cut out for you. Nursing that old man is *work*."

"I think it's stupid they wont let women be with him," said Evelyn. "Why it wouldn't bother me a bit to go down there and nurse my daddy. Wilgus honey, how do you want your eggs?"

"Would it bother all of you to shut your mouths a minute so Wilgus can tell us what the doctor said? I've been trying for half an hour to find out something factual about Daddy but I can't get a word in edgeways."

Grandma glared at Jenny. "Well now," she said. "Just who pulled *your* chain?"

Jenny started to cry. She jerked the cigarette out of her mouth, crushed it on top of the stove, then lifted one of the iron lids and threw the cigarette into the fire. She stood there holding the lid, glaring at Grandma through her tears.

"Mommy, I don't know what it is you lack, whether it's compassion, or common sense, or what. But Wilgus has been sitting there the last half-hour, trying to tell us some facts about Daddy. But has anybody in this house got sense enough to listen? Hell no."

"I've got sense enough to recognize somebody making a fool out of theirself," said Grandma.

Jenny's face turned red as she whirled around and banged the lid back down onto the stove. Then she whirled back and seemed close to throwing the coil-handled lifter right at Grandma. "That's right, Mommy," she snapped. "You go ahead. Put it all on me. Daddy's only lying down there on his deathbed. . . ."

"Jenny!" shouted Evelyn. "You hush that!"

"No," said Grandma calmly. "Let her go. Let her go ahead and show herself while Delmer and Wilgus is here to see. Just let her go."

"Actually," said Delmer, pushing his chair away from the table and standing up. "I've got to be going. In fact, Wilgus, you have to help me. My old generator's acting up this morning, I need you to run me to town."

"Why no!" Grandma protested. "This child has got to rest. He's been up all night, Delmer."

"He ain't even had his breakfast yet," said Evelyn. "I'm just about to fix him some eggs."

But I was glad to have an excuse to get away. I grabbed my coat and put it on as I followed Delmer out the back door, then around the house to where his truck was parked.

"My truck's okay," said Delmer. "I just figured you might like a graceful way out of the kitchen. That place can start to feel a little dangerous sometimes."

"Delmer, you're a wise, perceptive man."

"I know it," said Delmer. "And handsome too."

Delmer's spirit was so contagious I decided to drive him to town anyway, just to be with him a while longer. On the way we nipped from a bottle of whiskey he had in his pocket, and speculated on the outcome of the fight among the women back at the house.

"Let 'em fight," said Delmer. "It'll keep their minds off Daddy."

At the edge of town Delmer told me to pull in at the Chat 'N Chew. We had coffee and talked awhile. Before it was over Delmer had bought me a ham and egg breakfast and the morning Courier-Journal, and for a while he quit talking so I could read. I hadn't realized Delmer knew me that well, and I appreciated his gesture. By the time we got to the hospital I was feeling pretty good again.

Which was a good thing, because I wound up taking

care of Grandad again the rest of that day, and on into the night as well.

Boldly Delmer marched down the hospital corridor, cracking jokes as he took his coat off, getting ready for action.

But when he got his first good look at Grandad, lying perfectly still, his inflamed old eyes open wide, staring at the ceiling, Delmer turned pale and came very close to fainting. I drew up a chair for him, but he didn't stick around long enough to use it.

"Oh God," he moaned. "Oh God, he's dead. Look at him, Daddy's dead. Oh God."

On wobbly legs Delmer made his way back down the hall. I escorted him outside and stayed with him a few minutes while he breathed the fresh air and nipped some more from his whiskey bottle. But he was finished for the day. I gave him the keys to my car and he drove it home.

Later, Grandad asked me who it was that had made all that racket.

"That was Delmer, Grandad."

"Who?"

"Your son, Delmer."

The wrinkles in Grandad's forehead drew together as he stared at me suspiciously. "Whose side was he on?" he asked.

I laughed and fluffed his pillow for him, then helped him to lie back down.

65

"Well, Grandad, he was on their side. It's just me and you on this side now."

Grandad grinned. "Well," he said. "They're all spies anyway. False credentials. Fuzzy clouds and sweet-cold fire. Ain't that right?"

I pulled my chair to the side of his bed and flopped into it. "Yes sir, Grandad. That's right."

Grandad nodded as he relaxed into his pillow. "Furniture!" he yelled. "History! Sweet-cold fire!"

I yawned. Stretched. Nodded. "That's right, Grandad."

We closed our eyes and settled into our day together, dreaming of history and sweet-cold fire.

HOME FOR THE WEEKEND

If Junior hadn't said he liked Chevrolets better than Fords, the Collier family might have made it through the weekend without a fight.

But Junior said it, and as usual, his brother Delmer misunderstood.

"How come you know so much about it?" Delmer wanted to know. He'd been sipping moonshine. His face was red, and up close you could smell it on him.

"What do you mean?" said Junior.

"How come you to know so much about it?"

"About what, Delmer?"

"About cars, by god. You say Chevrolets is better than Fords. . . ."

"Why Delmer, I didn't say they were *better* than Fords. I just said I liked 'em better."

"Same damn difference," declared Delmer.

Junior didn't know what to say now, but it didn't matter because his wife Betty came in the kitchen about that time to say it for him.

"Damn it Delmer, it's okay to talk stupid, but why be so loud about it?"

Delmer looked at Betty, speechless. But he had a wife too, Pauline, out in the yard helping Grandma Collier peel potatoes.

"I'd talk if I was you Betty!" Pauline yelled through the window. "I can hear your big mouth plum out here!"

Betty's face turned red as Delmer's. She ran to the window, stuck her nose against the screen and in a nasal whine said, "An eavesdrop can hear anything, Pauline."

Pauline cursed, stabbed the ground with her butcher knife, jumped to her feet and charged around the house into the kitchen through the back door, just as cousin Richard and his wife, Evelyn and her husband L.C., Aunt Jenny, Grandma Collier, plus sundry children and grandchildren, all came flocking in from the living room.

The only one in the family who felt any impulse to go the other way was Wilgus. He was a college student, home, like the others, for Memorial Day weekend. Wilgus had grown up in that house on a diet of kinfolks fighting and he didn't have much appetite for it anymore. But before he could get away his Uncle L.C. cornered him between the cabinet and the coal stove and started yelling. Wilgus figured that if there wasn't any way to avoid foolishness the least he could do was elevate the tone of it. So he took a deep breath, looked L.C. in the eye, and declared that he thought strip mining was the work of the devil and that the whole coal industry ought to be nationalized.

"Why you goddamn . . . *beatnik*," L.C. snarled, just as Junior's wife Betty, who'd been shouting at Delmer, turned toward Wilgus and said, "For your information, Wilgus, I've got a brother working at a strip mine."

Wilgus started to ask what that had to do with it, but L.C. shook his finger in his face and said, "Why Wilgus, where do you think jobs around here would come from if it wasn't for strip mining? People has to *work*."

"By god, L.C.," Delmer shouted across the room. "They'd come from deep-mined coal like they always done. There'd be work aplenty if they'd stick to deep mines."

"Delmer, that's all well and good," said Junior. "But the thing is, they never would of started this strip mining if John L. Lewis had any guts."

Delmer choked. He grabbed somebody's ice tea off the table, downed about half of it, and when he got his voice back he looked Junior in the eye and said, "*What did you say?*"

"I said if John L. hadn't let us down, the miners could of taken the whole thing over by 1950, and *working* people would call the tune."

Junior and Delmer had been arguing about John L. Lewis since the strike of 1949. L.C. and Wilgus had heard it all many times before so they turned away to continue their quarrel in private just as Jenny, always the first to cry, started crying.

"If Mommy had taken Daddy to the hospital when I told her to, he'd be living yet," she whimpered.

"We ought to of lawed the bastards for every cent they had," said Evelyn.

"By God," Delmer shouted, "if the union had stuck together. . . ."

L.C. waved his arms in the air and said, "The Catholics and the Jews!"

"By god," Junior declared, "Chevrolets *is* better than Fords."

Betty told Pauline to shut up. Jenny told Betty to kiss her ass. Junior called L.C. a son of a bitch and Wilgus said goddamn. Delmer and L.C. were on their way outside to have a fistfight when old Grandma Collier told them all to hush their mouths.

"Just hush," she commanded, striding roughly through the crowd. "Not another word out of a one of y'uns, do you hear?"

For a long moment, the only sound in the kitchen was the hum of the old refrigerator.

Then Betty started crying too. "Come on Junior, we're going to Cincinnati."

70

"I'm going to North Carolina," Jenny wailed.

Evelyn told L.C. to round the children up, they were leaving for Perry County in five minutes.

Junior and Betty started for the door. But half way across the floor he remembered the ten dollars Delmer had owed him the last two years, and he decided to collect it. Everybody expected Delmer to say something awful to Junior but he didn't. Without batting an eye he counted out ten ones on the table. Then as an afterthought he took a handful of change out of his pocket, threw it on the floor at his brother's feet and said, "There's the goddamn interest."

"Well if that's the way of it," Evelyn said to Junior, "you can just pay me back for that tank of gas I bought."

"Gladly," said Junior. He handed Evelyn three of the ones Delmer had given him.

Suddenly everybody started remembering all the old, petty debts the others owed them. For the next few min utes the kitchen looked like the stock exchange. Nobody was shouting now. Everyone was grimly polite as they handed their money back and forth.

"Why thank you darling," Betty said as she collected a dollar and forty cents of the money Evelyn had just got from Junior that Junior got from Delmer, for a collect call Evelyn had made to Betty the week before. Delmer collected two dollars each from Junior and L.C. for the fishing licenses he'd paid for on a trip to Cherokee Lake.

Jenny collected a dollar each from Junior, Delmer, Evelyn, L.C. and Wilgus for their share of the cost of flowers
she'd bought on behalf of the family when Mr. Stidham
died. Then she turned around and gave Wilgus back his
dollar, plus two more to make up for the time he'd paid
the taxi fare the night her car broke down. Before Wilgus
got a good hold on the money though, Junior snatched it
out of his hand and said, "Remember that bet on the
Kentucky-Tennessee football game?"

It might have gone on all afternoon if Grandma Collier
hadn't started crying. But one by one they noticed that
she was. She wasn't yielding to her tears. She tried to keep
them back. She sat watching her thick hands nervously
toying with the salt shaker, now and then lifting her hand
to wipe away the tears. Gradually the moneychanging
died away and the kitchen grew quiet.

"I can't stand it," Jenny bawled. She started pushing
her way out of the room.

"I can't either," said Pauline, and she took off after
Jenny. A minute or two later Junior went along behind
them.

Delmer was the first of the men to start crying. His
outrage was spent now. He sniffed, wiped his eyes, and for
lack of anything else to do, he awkwardly edged up to the
table and laid his handful of money next to his mother's
arm.

Suddenly the old woman looked up, wiped her eyes,
and it was as if she hadn't been crying at all. Her voice was

clear and strong again as she looked from face to face, held out her hand and said, "Give it here!"

"Give it here!" she said more firmly when no one moved. "Put it ever bit right here on this table."

Everyone was so relieved she'd quit crying they fought each other to get up to the table and lay their money down. After Jenny and Pauline and Junior came back in and added their money to the pile, it totaled nineteen dollars and forty cents.

Betty leaned over and patted her mother-in-law on the arm. "You take that and buy yourself something nice."

"Hush your mouth," said the old woman. "I wouldn't keep it if it was a thousand dollars. Where's Wilgus at?"

"I think we ought to all spend it together," said Evelyn. "Let's all buy something together."

Jenny said she thought they ought to spend the money on flowers for their father's grave.

"Not nineteen dollars worth!" Pauline said before she could catch herself.

"I don't see why not," said Jenny. "I think our Daddy deserves the very best that we can give."

"Jenny, honey, the grave's knee-deep in flowers already," said Junior.

Jenny whirled around and glared at her brother. "Junior, I don't know about you, but I loved my daddy. He was the finest man that ever lived as far as I'm concerned."

"That's not what I mean," said Junior.

"Leave her alone," said L.C.

"Shut your mouth," Junior said to L.C.

"Shut yours," said Evelyn.

"I can't stand it," said Jenny, and she broke into tears again and would have left the room if her old mother hadn't shouted, "Never mind, never mind! Where's Wilgus at? I'm going to give this money to him. Come up here, Wilgus."

Wilgus came forward and without hesitation took the money, visions of spending it already forming in his mind. He'd buy watermelons with it. He'd host the entire family at a watermelon feast, outside in the yard. He'd jump in Delmer's Ford and run down to Godsey's store and get four of those big ripe melons just in from Georgia, and they would all gather in the yard and feast on them before they set out for their various destinations later in the day.

But that was a romantic vision, and terribly timed. His relatives had no patience for any watermelon feast this Memorial Day. Hastily they gathered up their children and piled into their cars, Wilgus among them as they drove down the Trace Fork road to the highway.

That's okay, Wilgus thought as he drove alone toward Lexington. There's other things to do with money. He would spend it on beer at the Paddock Club, share his windfall with his writer friends. And as they drank, he would tell them about his family in the hills, describe Memorial Day weekend with the clan. His friends might not believe the stories about his family, but still they would join him in a toast to their benefactors. "To the clan!" Wilgus would say, holding his glass aloft. And his pals would clink their glasses and drink together, and then say, "To the clan!"

THE REVIVAL

Wilgus found his Uncle Delmer sitting on the couch in the living room, staring at the wavy lines and falling snow on the silent television screen. Delmer held an open Bible in his lap and a king-size beer in his hand.

"Delmer old buddy, how you doing?" Wilgus asked as he sat down next to his uncle.

Delmer waited a long time before he answered. Without taking his eyes off the TV screen he said, "I ain't doing no good."

"You know who I am, don't you?"

Slowly, like an old turtle, Delmer turned his head. After studying his nephew's face a minute he said, "You're Wilgus, ain't you?"

Wilgus laughed and gave his uncle's knee a squeeze. "You're not as bad off as they said you were, Delmer."

But Delmer didn't laugh with Wilgus. He felt too awful to laugh. And he looked every bit as bad as he felt. Delmer was only forty-three, but after twenty-one straight days of hard drinking he looked more like sixty-three, and a sick sixty-three at that. His eyes were red and rheumy. The flesh around his nose was moist and raw-looking. Apparently he hadn't shaved since he'd started drinking. His cheeks were covered by a scraggly gray beard. His hair lay across his head in a tangle of oily gray matted strings.

"I'm bad off, all right," Delmer sighed.

"Well," said Wilgus. "I'm glad to see you sitting up, anyhow. From what they all said, I was afraid I'd find you stretched out on the floor or something."

Delmer sipped his beer, then sipped it again, each time carefully returning the hand that held the can back to the arm rest of the old stuffed couch.

Delmer and Wilgus watched TV a while without saying anything. Finally Delmer looked at his nephew and said, "I guess you know I'm hell-bound, don't you?"

"No," said Wilgus. "I didn't know that."

"I am," said Delmer. "My soul's blacker'n a piece of coal."

"Aw, Delmer. You don't mean that."

Delmer's eyes filled up with tears as he said, "I'm afraid Jesus ain't going to let me in."

Delmer turned his head away so Wilgus wouldn't see

his tears. In order to pretend he hadn't, Wilgus got to his feet and said, "It's cold in here, Delmer. I'm going to build us a fire."

Before he could build a fire Wilgus had to clean the ashes out of the bottom pan of the living room heater and carry them out to the ash pile in the back yard. While he was outside he split some kindling and filled a bucket with coal. As the wood and coal caught fire Wilgus went around the room picking up the empty beer cans and whiskey bottles that lay scattered across the floor and led away in trails toward the bedrooms and the kitchen. He filled a cardboard box five times with the litter, emptying it each time outside by the ash pile. By the time he'd swept the living room and kitchen floors the fire was going good in the heater and the room was beginning to warm.

"Delmer, how about something to eat?" Wilgus asked. "Little soup, or something."

Delmer shook his head forlornly.

"Food in your stomach might make you feel better."

"I don't *deserve* to feel no better," Delmer moaned. His voice collapsed in a fit of weeping as soon as the words were out of his mouth. He cried hard this time, not even trying to hide it. Wilgus turned and went back to the kitchen and began to rummage around for something to eat.

The only edible food in the house turned out to be a can of bean soup and two old heels of bread, plus a solitary beer in the far corner of the refrigerator. Looking around

79

to be sure Delmer didn't see him, Wilgus opened the beer and took a drink. He hid the can under a paper bag next to the breadbox and sipped from it as he worked in the kitchen, cooking soup and washing dishes. When the soup was ready he poured two coffee cups full and carried them into the living room.

"Delmer, here's some hot soup if you want it."

Delmer was staring at the TV screen again. He seemed to have forgotten all about his nephew being there with him. The Bible lay open on his lap now, and his hand rested on the page as if he'd been tracing words with his finger. When Wilgus thrust the cup in front of his face, Delmer dropped his eyes to look at it. Carefully he closed the Bible and laid it on the couch next to his leg. Then he accepted the steaming cup of soup with both hands.

They sipped their soup without talking. When the broth was gone they ate the beans with spoons. Delmer ate a lot slower than Wilgus but gradually he got it all down. When Wilgus offered him a second cup and a piece of hard bread to go with it, he took it, dipped it into the soup, then bit off the soggy end and chewed it slowly. When he swallowed he looked across at Wilgus and said, "I guess you heard about Pauline leaving me."

"Yeah, I heard about that, Delmer."

"Just up and went," said Delmer. "Took the children, took her clothes. Gone!"

"How come 'em to leave, do you reckon?" asked Wilgus.

"Ay, Lord," Delmer sighed. "Cause I'm so goddamn sorry, I reckon."

"You're not sorry, Delmer," said Wilgus.

"It's a punishment is what it is," said Delmer.

Wilgus asked Delmer who he thought was punishing him.

Delmer looked at his nephew through fresh tears. "God!" he said.

Wilgus scraped the remaining beans from his cup and ate them. As he stood up he said, "Well Delmer, I don't think God's going to punish you much longer. My feeling is, Pauline and the children'll be coming home before long. In fact, I wouldn't be surprised if they didn't come back some time tomorrow. The thing for me and you to do is clean the house up some before they get here. I've already started washing the dishes."

Wilgus took Delmer's empty cup and without further word went back to the kitchen where he went to work again on the great mound of dishes in the sink.

It took Delmer a full ten minutes to work his way off the couch and stagger into the kitchen to ask Wilgus what he'd said. He fell back twice, trying to rise. He finally had to get down on his knees and crawl along the floor a ways before he could maneuver his long body to a vertical position. But at last he made it. Supporting himself on the furniture as he walked, leaning against the walls and then the door frame at the entrance to the kitchen, Delmer at last arrived. His beer can was empty now, but he raised it to his lips and after blinking his eyes and stammering and stuttering awhile, he said, "What was that you said?"

"About what, Delmer?"

"About my wife Pauline."

"I just said she's coming home tomorrow, and me and you ought to straighten the house up some before she gets here."

"Coming here?"

"Yep. Be here in the morning. Going to bring the kids."

"Lord God." Delmer turned around and started back toward the couch in the living room. But half way there he turned again, nearly falling in the process, and went back to lean against the door frame.

"She ain't coming here?"

"Sure is," said Wilgus. "They'll all be here tomorrow."

"Lord God."

Delmer's face turned green as his beans bolted out of his stomach and flooded his throat and mouth. Pitching and falling, he lurched through the living room and down the short hallway to the bathroom, letting go of the beer can to hold both hands to his mouth as he ran. Some of the vomit went on the bathroom floor and some went down his shirt front. But most of it went in the commode as Delmer knelt in front of it and held his head close to the water.

Wilgus went on washing dishes as long as Delmer was authentically vomiting. But when his uncle's dry heaves

82

started he went to the bathroom and without a word set about scrubbing the dirty ring from the sides of the tub.

"Lorrd Gahd!" Delmer wailed between heaves.

"You'll be all right," Wilgus reassured him.

"Oh Lorrd Jesus Gahd!"

As the tub filled, Wilgus helped his uncle to his feet and out of his filthy clothes. All Delmer could say as he stepped into the steaming water was "Lorrd Gahd!"

But as Delmer began to wash himself in the tub, he found other things to say. "My children's like little angels to me," he said.

"They're good kids," said Wilgus.

"But what have they got for a daddy but a damned old devil."

"You're not a devil," said Wilgus. "You're a good man."

Wilgus was shampooing Delmer's hair now, scrubbing the scalp with his finger tips and running his fingers through the thickly lathered hair. The force of Wilgus' hands bent Delmer's head over until his chin nearly touched his chest. Yelling in order to be heard above the running water, Delmer shrieked, "I been reading the Bible!"

"I noticed you had it open," Wilgus yelled back.

"You know what it's been telling me to do?" Delmer yelled.

"What's that, Delmer?"

83

"It's been telling me to straighten up and do right!"

"That sounds like pretty good advice," said Wilgus.

He maneuvered his uncle to the front of the tub where he rinsed his head under the faucet. As Wilgus soaped his hair again and went on scrubbing, Delmer yelled, "I mean, a man's got to do *right*."

"He's got to try to, anyway," said Wilgus.

"If a man don't do right, he can't get no peace. Ain't that right?"

"That's right," said Wilgus.

He held Delmer's head under the faucet again. When he emerged, looking like a wet pup, Delmer looked up at Wilgus and said, "You know Jesus is the Prince of Peace, don't you?"

"Yeah, I know that," said Wilgus.

Wilgus had turned away to find Delmer's shaving gear. The razor was so full of gunk it took him a few minutes to get it clean in the sink, and to find a new blade. While he searched Delmer exclaimed, "Jesus offered peace to anybody that's got sense enough to take it, and brother I'll tell you now, them that don't take it's lost, ain't that right?"

"That's right," said Wilgus.

"I mean, they're gone!"

Wilgus covered Delmer's face with shaving cream. Yelling through the white foam, Delmer said, "I mean, you get to the forks of the road, you got to go one way or the other, you can't go but one way. You go down one road toward the devil, or down the other where Jesus is, ain't that right?"

"Amen," said Wilgus.

"Amen is right," said Delmer. "The devil's down one road, walking around like an old lion, ready to eat you. It says that in the Bible. But down the other road is Jesus, calling out to us to come home. He's *calling* us, brother. And when you feel the call you either go or you don't go, ain't that right?"

"That's right," said Wilgus. "Hold still now, I'm getting ready to shave off that beard."

Wilgus shaved one side of Delmer's face, then twisted his head around so he could shave the other.

"I've been hearing the call," said Delmer. "But I've just been too drunk to *answer*."

"Well, you're going to sober up now," said Wilgus.

"I'm going to sober up, and I'm going to start doing right," said Delmer. "Yes sir. I am."

After Wilgus finished the shave he helped Delmer out of the tub and handed him a towel. While his uncle dried himself Wilgus looked for clean underwear in the bedroom. He found some white longhandles in the bottom of the bureau and carried them in to Delmer. Dressed in them, his wet hair combed, his face smooth and shiny clean, Delmer looked like a brand new man.

But a very tired new man. His eyes were drooping shut

85

as he waited for Wilgus to put clean sheets on his bed. As Wilgus tucked him in, Delmer blinked and moved his lips to say something. But sleep was coming over him too fast for him to do more than mutter a faint amen.

Wilgus said amen.

Then he went in the living room to telephone his Aunt Pauline, and try to persuade her to come on home.

THE WOUNDED MAN

Wilgus is sitting at the kitchen table with a tape recorder in his lap, sipping hot chocolate which Aunt Evelyn has made on the electric stove across the room. There's a coal stove in the kitchen but it stands cold now. The season of fires indoors has passed, although hot chocolate in the evening after supper still feels good to the tongue. Evelyn's two small children have already been put to bed, but her two older ones are sitting at the table with their big cousin Wilgus, waiting for their grandmother to tell them the story of the wounded man. Evelyn has heard her mother tell the story many times over the years, but she's no less interested than the youngsters. When they have all been served hot chocolate, she pours herself a cup and takes her place at the table next to Wilgus, who is sitting

*at the corner nearest the old woman. Grandma Collier
knows her story is being tape recorded, and she's a little
nervous about it. She's willing, but she doesn't want to
see the machine as she talks so Wilgus has it on his lap
out of sight. The microphone is on a folded dish towel on
the table between him and his grandmother.*

*Grandma Collier sips her chocolate while the children
and grandchildren get situated at the table. When all
the shuffling and fidgeting are done, she clears her throat
and begins:*

I'd been outdoors all morning, I remember, making a
batch of soap in this big iron kettle I'd got for a wedding
present. I was still just a snip of a girl, nineteen years old,
going on twenty, but I knew how to do things, you ne'en
to worry yourself about that. I was strong. I could lift and
run and carry, I could work as good as any man. This par-
ticular morning I'd built me a good fire outside under my
kettle and I had my soap cooking nice. And I was standing
there above it, my head full of thoughts, you know how
you'll do when you get off by yourself working at something you don't have to pay much mind. I had me some
big-headed thought on my mind that occupied me and
the last thing in the world that I was expecting to see was
a strange man come walking out of the woods right there
into my yard.

We lived right in the very head of the holler, you see,
and we never saw anybody up there much except a few old

pack peddlers from time to time, and now and then some kind of candidate out lectioneering from house to house. Compared to what it is now it was pure wilderness on the creek. Our closest neighbor was a mile away and they was just a narrow little footpath through the woods unless you wanted to walk the creek bed. Oh, now, I don't mean to paint it blacker than it was. We lived good, had plenty to eat and kept warm in winter, and we'd see folks of a Sunday and down at the store when we'd go trade. All I mean to say is that it was just unusual for anybody to come back up the holler as far as our place, and I was mighty surprised when this man showed up, that's all.

He was dressed what you might say like a preacher dresses, or a politician. Had him a white shirt on, and black trousers and the shiniest black boots you ever saw. Ordinarily I would of been proud enough to have such a feller come to visit, only this one looked so wild-eyed and acted so crazy I got scared as soon as I seen him. He couldn't walk straight. Every step he took he pitched and heaved and stumbled around, about like those old drunks you see staggering out of saloons over in Blaine, and at first that's what I thought this feller was, just an old drunk, maybe a moonshiner, out lost in the woods. Of course I never had any idea that he'd been cut open and was about to bleed to death. His wound was in the back, you see, and from where I was standing, there by my fireplace next to the wash house, I couldn't see any sign of blood. As far as I could tell he was just an old drunk that might be dangerous to me and so I got right uneasy and figured I better get inside the house where the gun was before that feller got too close.

But don't you know, before I could take a step, he fell over flat on his face, right there in my yard. Him laying there, worming around, moving and heaving, I seen that his back was bloody all over and well, I thought that he was sure a dead man, and for a little bit I didn't know but what I was going to just keel over in a faint right beside him. I had to fight to keep from running off into the woods. But finally I did manage to get hold of myself enough to go find out if he was dead or not. I felt of his neck and found a pulse, and I seen him still bleeding. Blood pumped through his shirt and shined in the sun like new house paint. I knew I had to do something to help him, stop his bleeding, get him inside somehow. But I also knew I couldn't do it by myself. So I begun to yell for Dad. Dad! Dad! Come quick! I yelled.

Actually I didn't call him Dad then. We hadn't been married a year. I was carrying Wayne but just barely, I don't even think I was sure I was going to have a baby yet. Maybe I just suspected it. Anyhow, Herschel is what I yelled. Herschel! Herschel! Come quick! Directly here he come a running. He'd been digging postholes the far side of the property some place. I remember he had his diggers with him when he got to the yard. When he saw me bent over that wounded man he give them diggers a pitch and pushed me to one side and picked that man up in his arms and carried him face down all the way to the house without stopping.

Dad was strong as a bull when he was young. He was a logger before he become a miner, he had arms big around as your leg in them days. He was a powerful thing. I had to run to keep up with him, he was traveling so fast. Without saying a word to one another we went straight to the kitchen table. I cleaned it off in a swipe and Dad cased the feller down on his belly. Then in another swipe I stripped his shirt off and there that big cut was, the awfullest sight I'd ever seen in all my life. It was eleven inches long by measurement. And he was breathing through his cut! Sucking air in right through the wound! Beat all I ever seen. When he'd take in air it seemed like the blood would slow a little. But then when he'd let it out here the blood would come again. In and out, in and out went the feller's air, right through the hole in his back, breathing through his lights.

He couldn't have had more than a teacup of blood left in him. His flesh was cold and drained, he was white as a corpse already. I didn't see no way for that man to live, but of course they wasn't anything to do but try to save him. I run to the chest and got one of my new sheets, ripped me off a big section, soused it down in the drinking water and squeezed it out and bent over the man and commenced to wipe the blood away. I messed and gommed around on him for two or three minutes before that wound laid open and free. The blood seemed to slow down then, and for a minute I thought I'd saved him, thought it was going to be that easy. But I was hasty, for pretty soon here that old blood come again, lifting up in a pool down inside the wound and flowing over the sides across his back. It was awful. And about that time the man give a wrench, too, the first time he'd moved since we got him inside. And he made this noise out of his mouth. It almost made me sick. And poor Dad, strong a man as he was, he had to go outside and puke it made him so sick. But at least the man's movement showed there was life yet in him, so I knew I had to keep on working. I tore me off another piece of sheet and wadded it against the wound and pressed it down. And Dad come back in and both of us pressed rags against the feller's back hard as we could press. My hand was against the rags, and Dad's hand was over my hand and my other hand was over his hand, locked together. We pressed against that wound, it seemed like hours to me. For awhile I thought we was doing some good and I said to myself, God wants this feller saved. He's going to save him. But pretty soon here the blood come again, right on through, all over my hand and onto Dad's hand, till finally we had to give it up when the rags got soaked with blood.

Lord help him, I said. He's gone for sure now. And all of a sudden I bust out crying. There didn't seem to be anything else to do. I just sit back and let the old tears come.

It was something, the kind of feeling I had then. It works on me now just thinking about it. I believed for sure that death was about to enter my house and I felt just useless to stop it, and tired, and crying and I don't know, just gone plum crazy I reckon.

And Dad, he was crazy too. When we couldn't do no good fighting that blood he took a crazy running fit, run out the door and across the yard, got half way to the forks of the road before he knew what he was doing. He said he'd never felt so crazy and scared and sick all at the same time as he did then. Even in later years, after he seen awful things happen to men in the mines, men killed, crushed under big rocks, suffocated, Dad said there never was anything happened that was as awful to him as that wounded man bleeding to death on our table, never a feeling as terrible as the one he had, running to get a doctor knowing that the man had to be dead before he could ever get back with one.

Well Dad didn't feel a bit worse than I did, let me tell you. When he run off down the creek and left me alone with that wounded man, shuddering and crying and generally give out and quit, I didn't think I'd ever live long enough to feel like my old real self again. I wanted to pray, I tried to pray. But I just didn't have one grain of faith that there was anything on earth that even God could do to save that man. I lost my faith completely, and that made me feel darker than ever. By then I didn't know

93

what was going to come of any of us and I was scared, oh Lord, I was scared.

But then, it was a real strange thing. I was sitting there all bowed over, sniffling and carrying on, scared and crying, sick. But then all at once I heard this noise across the room. It sounded like something rustling around in fodder, or like when you hear little mice gnawing between the walls at night, scratchy-like noises. I looked around, and I listened. And I felt something come over me. It seemed like something had come in the room, like all of a sudden I could feel something else in there with me and that wounded man. My first thought was that he'd sure enough died, that it was his ghost in the room, rustling around, trying to get out. But no. I could see the man still breathing, and I felt of him and he still had a pulse. And then I heard the sound again. It was like it had a power to it that pulled me across the room, right over to the wall where the chimley was. I stood there real still, trying to listen. I commenced looking all around for what was making that noise. I looked and I looked, everywhere along the wall I looked to find what was making that noise. But all I could see was my same house, my same fireplace with the same cold ashes in it, and it was just the queerest feeling I ever had, for my house to look so familiar to me and yet feel that different. I felt like running out of there and never going back again. I wanted to run off from that place and just keep on going and going. But I never. I took up the poker and stirred the ashes a time or two, hunting, expecting that something might run out, hoping almost that it would.

And children, if I wasn't a Christian before then I surely was afterwards, and forever more. For what I remembered when I looked at that fireplace and chimley was sut. Lordy, mercy me. Quick as I could I run back across the room to where the wounded man was on the table and stripped them bloody old rags off his back. Then I run back to the chimley and grabbed me up a big double-handful of sut, and I dobbed that cut in his back as full of it as I could dob. I made two trips to the chimley and back, and I reckon I stuffed that feller full. And don't you know that it wasn't more than a few minutes before that sut turned into the thickest mud that the blood couldn't come through. That sut stopped that old blood from flowing out, and I swear if it wasn't but another minute or two before that feller commenced to get a little of his natural color back. By the time Dad and the doctor got there, the man's flesh had got warm again, and you could just see the life building up in him.

Dad had been gone four hours by then. I'd lost all sight of time myself, but that's how long he said it had been. He wouldn't of got back nearly that fast if he hadn't run into old Doctor Spurlock on the road half way to town. Dad had run three miles down the creek to the store, and got a horse there and set out for Blaine on it, and then met the doctor on the way. Doc had been out all the night before, helping a Landrum girl have a baby on Second

Creek. He was on his old sway-back mare. They hurried up Trace Fork to our house, expecting to find me there with an old corpse on my hands.

By then of course I looked more like a corpse than the wounded man did. I had sut and blood to my elbows and sut all over my face. My hair was down in my eyes, I looked like I'd been in war. And do you know, even with that poor man laying there at death's door, still yet the thing that was on my mind was how embarrassed I was to have Doctor Spurlock see me like that. But he bragged on me. He said. Mrs. Collier—that's how he talked; always formal and polite although I was still just a girl to him—he said, I guess you know you saved this man's life. I looked at him and says back to him, no, Doctor, it wasn't me. God is the one that saved that man. God was watching over him. He showed me what to do and all I did was do it, that's all. Well, old Doc, he grinned right big and he patted me on the shoulder and he said well Mizz Collier, anyway, you done good. If that sut don't poison him or turn him into a nigger, I believe he'll be okay.

Well, you know, I *had* done good. I didn't claim any credit for saving that wounded man. I'd give up on him and I'd lost my faith, and it was only God's power that reminded me about that sut and saved him. But still yet, I knew I'd done good. It was the most wonderful feeling in the world to know that there wasn't going to be an old dead man in our house before my baby was born.

Plenty of death come later, of course. We lived in that

house fourteen years before it burnt. Had eleven younguns there. Two died as babies. They're buried back up on the hill, been there fifty years and more by now. Glen and Anna Dean, and poor little Wayne, killed in war. And then Dad. He's up there with them now. There's been plenty of death in our family all right.

But I've got six yet living! And all you little 'uns. Everybody's scattered, but they're doing good. I'm proud of 'em, ever one. And we all get together at Christmas time, and Decoration Day, they're all here. We keep the graveyard nice. I'm proud about that.

As for that old wounded man. He was a real mystery. He was strange. Do you know what he did? That scoundrel. He got up and left our house before it was even time to take the stitches out. He laid there nine days, then just got up and left. Name of Murdock, from Breathitt County. He said he'd come up through Finley on his way to Leslie County to court some gal, said he took the shortcut up through Trace Fork is how come he passed by our land. Said he was on his way home when he got waylaid there at the head of the holler just off our property. He didn't like to talk about it. He was polite enough and always grateful for anything you done for him. But he wouldn't tell us much about his fracas except to say that two men had done it, and left him for dead.

But anyway, ten days after he staggered into our yard nigh dead, he got up out of bed, borrowed a suit of Dad's clothes and walked off the way he'd come. We never did hear of Murdock anymore, except when he sent Dad's clothes back by mail.

And that's the story of the wounded man, the best I recollect it.

MAXINE

Maxine had ridden the bus eleven hours, from Detroit to Blaine, Kentucky, and by the time her cousin Wilgus met her at the station she was exhausted. She was a little hysterical too after the week she'd just spent with her daughter Cindy, so at the edge of town Wilgus went in a liquor store and bought Maxine a bottle of Mogen David to drink as he drove her home.

"Cindy was living in the dingiest goddamn hotel I ever seen," said Maxine. "No windows, no bathroom, no nothing. Damn baby due. Had three dollars when I got there. And that sorry Billy nowhere in sight."

She sipped the wine and handed the bottle to Wilgus. Wilgus didn't feel like drinking, particularly Mogen

David, but he took a sip to be companionable and handed the bottle back to Maxine.

"Cindy knew where the little son of a bitch was at, but she didn't want to tell me," Maxine went on. "I reckon she's afraid I'd kill him. Said she'd changed her mind about Billy. Said they'd made up, was going to work things out together. Calls and gets me to come all the way to Detroit, then when I get there, tries to act like it ain't none of my business. Like the thing for me to do is just get back on the bus and go home. Her sitting there with that little round belly, face all lean, I swear Wilgus, she looked like some kind of war orphan."

Maxine sipped her wine.

"So where was Billy?" asked Wilgus.

"This other hotel, three blocks away. I went and found him, I told him if he didn't get Cindy out of that hotel to a better place, and get hisself a job, and generally treat my youngun better, I'd stick him in jail 'til he never got out. I told him if he run off from Cindy anymore I'd hunt him down and cut his goddamn guts out. I's so mad, I could of killed him right there."

Maxine took another drink of wine, then lit a cigarette. But after three puffs she put it out and went on talking.

"So anyway, it took us all week, but I reckon they're finally settled. It ain't much of an apartment but at least it's got a bathroom in it. Billy went to work for Manpower, I reckon he'll stick at it a month or two."

"I thought Billy was going to turn out better than that," said Wilgus.

"Shit," Maxine snorted. "If Cindy was looking for something worthless to take up with, she sure found it."

Maxine sipped the wine and handed the bottle to Wilgus and this time he took a good long drink.

They were driving along the Rock Creek road, headed east toward Bonnet Creek where Maxine lived, twenty-five miles from Blaine. The road through the Rock Creek valley was paved but it was so narrow there was barely room for two cars to pass. Every few miles Wilgus had to ease the car half off the road to let a coal truck pass, twenty-ton empties, most of them, the drivers headed home after their last run to the loading ramps at Champion. Except for the trucks there was very little traffic on the road. And by the time they got to Whitaker Crossroads, half way between Blaine and the mouth of Bonnet Creek, there weren't very many people outside either. The first few miles out of town they had seen people working in their gardens or sitting on their porches, raising their hands in greeting as they passed by. But it was nearly dark now. The valley was filling with the shadows of the hills that rose on either side of Rock Creek. A mile beyond the Crossroads, Wilgus turned his headlights on. Then he reached over and put his arm around his cousin and drew her to him.

To help Maxine get her mind off her troubles, Wilgus

started talking about the trip he was going to take to California later in the month. Wilgus had graduated from the University a few weeks before. He planned to go back in the fall to graduate school. Before settling in for another round of study he wanted to change his pattern for awhile, get away from books, away from Kentucky, have an adventure off someplace he'd never been before. To set forth in his car and head west with no precise plan or destination was unlike anything Wilgus had ever done before, and the prospect of the journey had filled his mind ever since school was out.

"Yeah," said Maxine when Wilgus had outlined his scheme. "I know what you're going to do. You're going to get out there to California and forget to come back. Homefolks'll never see you again."

Maxine made her remark jokingly but Wilgus was serious when he answered. "No," he said. "I'm coming back."

Maxine sipped her wine. "Well," she said. "I wouldn't blame you if you never come back to this place. If I could go with you I sure as hell wouldn't come back."

"Now there's an idea," said Wilgus. "Why don't you come along? We'd have a fine old time."

"Maybe I could find me a cowboy out there to marry," Maxine laughed. She sipped her wine. "Ay, Lord," she muttered, "I pity any cowboy that'd take up with the likes of me."

"He'd be a lucky cowboy," said Wilgus.

Maxine grunted, and drank more wine. "No," she said. "I don't want no cowboy. But I would like to go out there and see the sights someday."

"What I want to see is the Grand Canyon," said Wilgus.

"Lord, honey, don't take me to no canyons," said Maxine. "If I's at a canyon I'd dive off head first into the damn thing and be done with it."

"No, now," said Wilgus. "I wouldn't let you do that. What we'd do is walk down in it. Go exploring. We could ride those burros they've got. . . ."

"Lord God!" Maxine laughed, sitting up suddenly. "Don't put me on donkeys! I look foolish enough as it is. I'll soon be a *grandma*, Wilgus."

"The Lone Grandma," Wilgus teased. "Get you a mask, a white burro. . . ."

"*Hush!*"

But Maxine couldn't help laughing at the image and Wilgus laughed with her. They both took a drink of wine.

"Maybe that's what I ought to do," said Maxine after a while. "Get me a gun and a mask and go around killing my enemies. Anybody that pissed me off, I'd shoot 'em down."

"And justice would be done," said Wilgus. "You'd feel *good* about it."

"I'd shoot Billy Dixon's ass plum off," said Maxine. "And then there's one or two on Bonnet Creek I'd like to

103

kill. Kill me a couple of strip miners. Few sons of bitches over at the courthouse. When it was over I'd shoot myself. Blow my brains out with a big ol' .44."

"No, now Maxine. You don't want to do that."

Maxine sipped her wine. "Don't bet on it," she said.

When they left the county pike and headed up the unpaved road that ran beside Bonnet Creek, they fell silent for awhile. Wilgus drove in first gear as he maneuvered the car around the larger rocks and deeper ruts of the narrow lane. In the old days, when Maxine was a child on Bonnet Creek, the highway department had maintained their road as well as any in the county. But after the ridges above the valley were strip-mined and the creek began to lose its population, the people who remained were lucky if the county graded their road every other year. In the winter only vehicles with four-wheel drive could make it as far as Maxine's house. Wilgus' Ford was making it now only because it was July and the road had been baked hard by the sun. Every half mile or so the road crossed the creek and in places ran in the creekbed several yards before rising on the other side. In the dark it took them half an hour to drive the four miles from the highway to Maxine's house near the head of the hollow. Neither spoke until Wilgus pulled up in front of the house and said, "Well, here we are."

I reckon so, said Maxine.

At least she thought she said it. She was so weary and

disoriented after her long day's journey she wasn't sure if she had spoken out loud or merely thought the words.

"Everything looks all right," said Wilgus. "At least nobody burned your house down while you were gone."

I wouldn't care if they had, Maxine thought.

"Did I say that?" she asked.

"What?" asked Wilgus.

Maxine didn't answer immediately. After staring out the window at the dark, familiar shape of her house she said, "This place feels like the end of the world to me."

"It's the same old Bonnet Creek," said Wilgus.

Not the same, Maxine thought.

"Did I say that?" she asked.

"About the end of the world?" asked Wilgus.

"Something."

Maxine was too tired to go on with the thought. She was so tired she couldn't even tell if she was crying or not. It felt as if she was. But somehow she didn't seem to be making any sound, and there weren't any tears in her eyes. But her shoulders were shaking and when Wilgus noticed that they were, he slid across the seat and put his arms around her, a full hug this time. Maxine leaned into his side without restraint and felt her tears begin. For a long time she cried in Wilgus's arms like a baby. As she cried she pictured Cindy as a baby, crying in her arms. Briefly Maxine dreamed she *was* Cindy, come home with Wilgus to Bonnet Creek again.

But as Wilgus helped her out of the car, it was only her same old self who was home.

"It's just me, folks," she sang out in the dark as Wilgus led her across the yard. "Just old stupid Maxine."

"You're a wonderful Maxine," Wilgus whispered.

A left-over piece of shit is all I am, Maxine thought.

"I didn't mean that," she said out loud.

"Shhh," said Wilgus. "It's okay."

Wilgus helped her up the steps and across the porch to the front door. Then, his arm around her waist, her head upon his shoulder, they entered the dark and airless house and made their way along the hall to the back bedroom. Fumbling in the dark, they found the bed and sat down on the edge.

"If I was Cindy and we all loved me," Maxine sang as Wilgus took off her shoes.

"Shhh," said Wilgus. "Be quiet, now."

"What all have I said?"

"Nothing, honey. Hold still now."

Maxine felt her cousin's hands unbutton her blouse and slip it off her arms. She felt him lay her on the bed and unzip her slacks, then slip them off her legs. She felt his good warm hands upon her legs and arms and shoulders as he pushed her into the center of the bed. Then she felt him lie down on the bed beside her and take her in his arms.

Oh lover, Maxine thought.

"I didn't mean," she said, startled, drawing away.

"Shhh," said Wilgus. "Just be still. It's all okay."

Maxine hugged her cousin's arm against her breasts. "I love you," she said out loud.

"And I love you," she heard him say. "You sleep now." And dream.

Maxine dreamed Wilgus kissed her on the mouth. She dreamed he touched her breast, then stroked her face with his hand. Then she dreamed she heard his car start up outside. As she listened to its sound grow fainter down the hollow, Maxine dreamed that she was with him, that she was Cindy, riding away with Wilgus, headed west, somewhere.

A CORRESPONDENCE

Dear Brother Luther,

I know you will be surprised to hear from me it's been so long. How I found out you was yet living and where, was Wilgus Collier is from there, who came to rent my upstairs apartment, a nice young traveling man. He says he grew up within a mile of where your daughter lives in Knott County, that his aunt is her neighbor and for you to tell her hello. I call it the Lord's miracle that He sent Wilgus Collier to my house a messenger of the only good news I have had in many years. I pray to Him this will reach you and that you will answer and we will be in touch with one another again.

So it's been many years since we were all at home together hasn't it dear Brother? I often think of those old days and wish I was back at home with my loved ones instead of sitting in this lonesome place by myself. Did you know I lived in Phoenix? I have lived here eleven years. My husband Troy bought this house with two apartments and one other with three apartments and moved us here in 1954 when he retired and for my asthma. Then the next year he died of heart trouble and Bright's disease so I have a mighty load to carry by myself. Troy had a boy and girl by his first marriage but they have forgot their old stepmother, and I never had children of my own as you perhaps know. It is lonesome in Phoenix and I breathe with difficulty, and my tenants are the only ones I see and they are not always friendly except Wilgus Collier, a nice young traveling man who the Lord sent to me and put me in touch with you again and oh I hope how soon we can be together again dear Brother, like we were so many years ago when we lived on Cowan Creek. Join me in thanks to God and write soon.

Your loving sister,
Mrs. Drucilla Cornett Toliver

Sweet Sister,

Could not believe your letter at first. I thought it was another trick to torment me. I read it, read it again, then had daughter Cleo read it to me to be sure it was true. A big surprise, to think for years I have a sister living after all.

Yes, many years have gone under the bridge since we were all at home together and so happy. Now everything is down to a final proposition it appears like. I have the gout and cataracts. My wife Naomi died two years ago. My younguns are scattered here and yon, except daughter Blanche who died and son Romulus who lost his mind. I live first with one then the other, but mostly daughter Cleo, the others don't want me much. Bad business to be amongst ungrateful children.

Arizona. A mighty fine place I hear. Your man done good by you to leave you so well off. I seen Goldwater on television one night, speaking right from Phoenix. He strikes me as a scoundrel but it showed pictures of fine Arizona country, the desert and the sunset on some mountains so peaceful and quiet, it sure looked like where I want to be. And I hope how soon we can be together sweet sister, to keep each other company in these terrible times.

Your brother Luther Cornett,
Age 79 how old are you by now?

Dear Brother,
I am 72. I have asthma and artherites, bursitis and awful high blood pressure. My fingers hurts now to write this letter and I hope you will be able to read it.

But you have a nice hand write, Brother. You always was a good scholar at Little Engle School. I remember walking to school with you boys, and the way it set back against the hillside, the front end of it on stilts high enough to play under, and the way the willows and the sycamores leaned out over Engle Creek, and wading the creek and the Big Rock we played on that had mint growing around it. I remember an Easter egg hunt at the school. And the fight you had with Enoch Singleton. I know I have forgot a lot of old times but I do remember that school very well and hope to see it when I get back to dear Kentucky.

Which should not be too long now. My houses are not fancy but they are buying up property right and left here and I have buyers galore to pick from. But I want to get a good price so we can afford ourselves a nice place together somewhere there in Knott County. Do you ever hear of any places for sale in the Carr Fork section? Who owns the old homeplace now? Maybe we could buy it back and live there again and be like we used to be so many years ago.

I look forward to meeting your Cleo and all your grandchildren. You are so lucky to have grandchildren. I never did even have children but I guess I told you that. Until I learned you were yet living I cried myself to sleep every night with only Jesus for my comfort. But now he has sent me you, and soon we will be re-united in His love, sweet Brother.

In His Holy Name,
Drucilla Toliver

Sweet Sister,

So much racket going on here I can't hardly think what to write. It is this way all the time in this house, no peace and quiet. Cleo won't control her younguns. They all promised me my own room before I moved in, but then never give me one, it was all a lure and a trap. I turn the television up full blast to drown them out. After a while you don't hear a loud television but it is still a poor substitute for true quiet like you all must have out west.

The '27 flood got Engle School.

A flood can come and get the rest of this place for all I care. Kentucky is all tore up and gone, Sister. Soon they'll flood Carr Fork and that whole section, including the old homeplace, the government's doing it. You are fortunate to have your property. I used to have property on Hard-burly Mountain, two hundred acres, with a good stand of white pine plus a well, dwelling house, barn and good-sized garden. But the strip miners got it all. I lawed the sons of bitches but couldn't do no good. So here I am stuck at Cleo's house, crowded up, no privacy, she can't cook, younguns gone wild, not enough heat, and they read my mail before I get it. (You be careful what you say!) Count your blessings in Arizona, sister, none in Kentucky to count. And keep your property, I'll be out there before long to help you run it and we'll get along good for ever more.

Your loving brother,
Luther

Dear Brother,

You would not like Arizona. It is not green and cool here like Kentucky, and Phoenix is difficult of living. I can't tell you too much about Phoenix except that Carson Avenue is a terrible place. I've only seen the downtown part once, in 1956 when the Presbyterians took me down and back one day for a good deed, but it wasn't much then and I doubt that it's any better now.

I want to pick blackberries again, and gather chestnuts and see the laurel when it blooms. I never see anything on Carson Avenue except the motorcycle gang go by. Taxes are awful and the heat and when you call the water company it takes it a month to come, and you can't see television because of this sarcastic neighbor Mr. Ortiz who pranks with the electricity.

So I'll be home in a month or two, soon as I settle up my business. You look for us a place to buy. Get it in the country, pick us out a cove off one of those cool hollows and have laurel on it if you can. It would be good to live close to Carr Creek or Troublesome, or maybe even over on North Fork River. I'm not much of a fisherman but you always were and I can cook fish. It would be handy if we could buy us a good house already built. But if you feel up to it, and some of your children would help, I'd like to buy a hillside with good timber on it and we could have us a house built out of our own wood, to suit us, and cheaper too. Wouldn't that be something? I'd like to be on the road to see people go by, nice Kentucky neighbors and kinfolks. Last Sunday I was sitting on my porch and a motorcycle man yelled an ugly thing at me and upset me terrible.

And I didn't exactly admire your using bad language in your last letter, Brother. That indicates you might not be saved, but I pray you are, but if you aren't tell me the truth about it.

Sister Drucilla

Drucilla,

Don't come to Kentucky. I tell you this is a terrible place. The union has pulled out. No work anywhere. They're gouging the hillsides down, stripping and auguring. Ledford Pope's house got totally carried off by a mudslide. The streams are fouled, not a fish this side of Buckhorn Lake, not even any water to speak of except at flood time when there's more than anybody wants. The young folks have mostly moved to Ohio and Indiana to work, and them that's left have no respect for old people, they'd never help us build a house even if we had something to build it out of. Kentucky's timber has been gone since you have. Coal trucks make more racket than motorcycles, and there's no air fit to breathe for the slate dumps burning. Sure no place for asthma sufferers.

I've seen the pictures of Arizona, and read about it. It sounds like all the old folks in the country are retiring out there but me. Damn such business as that, I'm on my way

x

soon as I can accumulate trainfare. If you've got some extra to send me for expenses I'd be grateful to you, and make it up to you once I got there. I'll rent two apartments from you myself, I want me some room to stretch in. And don't worry about getting downtown. Me and you will take right off the first thing and see all the sights and visit all the retired people in Phoenix and go to shows and ride buses and sit around the swimming pools drinking ice tea.

Sorry for the bad words. Yes, I'm saved. I was a terrible rip-roarer most of my life, but 12 years ago I seen the light and give up all bad habits except cussing. I'm ready to give that up too but see no way to go about it till I get somewhere where there ain't so much to cuss about.

Your brother,
Luther

Brother,

I'm not going to live in Arizona. That's all there is to it. You don't understand how it is here. Why do you not want me to come home? Are you making up all those bad tales on Kentucky, just to keep me from coming? I don't understand your attitude. A man that would cuss his sister would lie to her too, and the Bible admonishes against oaths and lies. I don't want to boss you but I'll not be bossed myself, and I absolutely will not stay in Arizona.

Drucilla Toliver

Sister,

You say you don't understand my attitude. Well I don't understand a sister that would have two fancy houses and yet turn out a suffering brother to suffer at the hands of mean children and a bad location. You talk like such a Christian. I say do unto others as you want them to do unto you and you're the one with two houses. I didn't cuss you. And I just wonder who is lying to who, for I have seen the pictures of Arizona and read of everybody moving there to retire and be happy. It sounds like you're all out there together plotting to keep me out. Well you won't get away with it and I have one question to ask: have you been getting secret letters from Cleo on the side? It wouldn't surprise me.

Luther Cornett

Brother,

I still refuse to stay in Arizona, in spite of your insults, and I suggest you read The Beatitudes.

Drucilla Cornett Toliver

Sister,

You and Cleo think you can lure and trap me into staying in Kentucky but you are wrong.

Luther Cornett

Luther,

You have turned out strange is all I can say, unmindful of the needs of others, and if you continue to curse me we might as well forget the whole business.

Drucilla Cornett Toliver

Drucilla,

I have not cussed you but I am about to get around to it. And Cleo and Emmit and Polly and Sarah and R.C. and Little Charles too if they all don't hush their racket. If you don't agree to my coming there then you are right, we might as well forget the whole thing for I absolutely refuse to stay in such a goddamn hell-hole as this.

Luther Cornett

Dear Luther,

Satan moves your tongue and I won't listen, or agree to stay here another week.

Drucilla Toliver

Dear Drucilla,

Then we just as well forget the whole thing.

Mr. Luther O. Cornett

Luther,
    Suit yourself.

                        Mrs. Drucilla Toliver